NEW YORK REVIEW BOOKS
C L A S S I C S

MACHINES IN THE ...

ANNA KAVAN (1901–1968) was born Helen Woods to wealthy British parents in Cannes. The family moved often between Europe and the United States and, when she was ten, Kavan was sent to boarding school in the United Kingdom. The following year her father committed suicide. In 1920, Kavan married a railway engineer and the two moved to Burma, where their son, Bryan, was born. The couple separated in 1925, and she returned to London to attend art school and began using heroin. In 1928 she married the artist Stuart Edmonds, and the next year published her first novel, *A Charmed Circle*. While married to Edmonds, she published six books as Helen Ferguson, and in 1935 they had a daughter, Margaret, who died shortly after birth. They soon adopted a daughter, Susanna. In 1938, as the marriage deteriorated, Kavan attempted suicide and was admitted to a psychiatric clinic in Switzerland. Adopting the name Anna Kavan (after a character who had appeared in two of her earlier books), she would write about this experience in the short-story collection *Asylum Piece* (1940), which was met with acclaim. She would go on to write criticism, journalism, dozens of stories, and several novels as Kavan, including her most successful book, the novel *Ice* (1967), which was published the year before she died of heart failure.

VICTORIA WALKER teaches in the English Department of Queen Mary, University of London, and chairs the Anna Kavan Society. She has published on twentieth-century women's writing and is currently working on the first critical study of Kavan.

MACHINES IN THE HEAD

Selected Stories

ANNA KAVAN

Edited by

VICTORIA WALKER

NEW YORK REVIEW BOOKS

New York

THIS IS A NEW YORK REVIEW BOOK
PUBLISHED BY THE NEW YORK REVIEW OF BOOKS
435 Hudson Street, New York, NY 10014
www.nyrb.com

The stories in this anthology were first published in volume form in Great Britain in 2019 by Peter Owen Publishers.

Library of Congress Cataloging-in-Publication Data
Names: Kavan, Anna, 1901–1968, author. | Walker, Victoria (Victoria Carborne) editor.
Title: Machines in the head : selected stories / by Anna Kavan, edited by Victoria Walker.
Description: New York City : New York Review Books, [2019] | Series: New york review books classics
Identifiers: LCCN 2019038488 (print) | LCCN 2019038489 (ebook) | ISBN 9781681374147 (paperback) | ISBN 9781681374154 (ebook)
Classification: LCC PR6009.D63 A6 2019 (print) | LCC PR6009.D63 (ebook) | DDC 823/.912—dc23
LC record available at https://lccn.loc.gov/2019038488
LC ebook record available at https://lccn.loc.gov/2019038489

ISBN 978-1-68137-414-7
Available as an electronic book; ISBN 978-1-68137-415-4

Printed in the United States of America on acid-free paper.
10 9 8 7 6 5 4 3 2

CONTENTS

FOREWORD

I can't keep on all my life writing in the same way...The world now is quite different and so is my life in it. One reacts to the environment and atmosphere one lives in, one absorbs outside influences, and my writing changes with the conditions outside.*

ANNA KAVAN BEGAN LIFE as a fictional character, the heroine of minor novelist Helen Ferguson's *Bildungsroman, Let Me Alone* (1930). Ten years later her author began to publish under the name of her former protagonist, taking the name Anna Kavan as her own. This shift from literary character to living writer reflects significantly on Kavan's writing, for the complexity of the relationship between reality and fiction is a preoccupation of her novels, stories and journalism. One of the few constancies of her writing after her name change was her determination to experiment, something that did not always make her work popular in her lifetime. Her own description of her writing practice above – 'I can't keep on all my life writing in the same way' – lays out her motives for this tendency towards change. When she began writing as Anna Kavan, Helen Ferguson's style underwent its first dramatic shift: her characters became nameless and enigmatic, her plots became scanty and her themes inclined towards darkness, fantasy, madness and dystopia. But she did not abandon

*Letter to Peter Owen, 29 March 1966, Harry Ransom Center, Austin, Texas.

realism, returning to her earlier style in several of her later novels and often writing in her own particular, peculiar hybrid of realism and fantasy. She was well aware that there was limited appetite for what she called 'my sort of experimental writing', but despite decades of difficulty getting her work into print she refused to replicate the style that had brought her literary success in the 1940s, preferring always to try something new or to rework a previous mode of writing. This shifting style and her long publishing career (which lasted from 1929 to 1967) make it difficult to understand her work within any particular tradition, and critics have sometimes accused her of writing only and obsessively about herself. But to consider her fiction outside the literary and intellectual climate of its times is to miss much of its value; in her terms the 'environment and atmosphere' she lived in shaped her writing. Reading stories brought together from across her career, as in this collection, illustrates how Kavan's fiction was shaped by the major social, political and cultural upheavals of the mid-twentieth century as much as by her personal experiences of mental illness, drug addiction and heartbreak.

Kavan's deliberate neglect of fictional plot and character development seems to have encouraged an impulse to embellish her life story, and during the fifty years since her death her biography has been expansively embroidered. She was born Helen Woods in Cannes in 1901, the only child of affluent British parents, and named Helen after her mother. Their wealth must have dwindled, for when Helen was a small child they moved from Somerset to Rialto, California, to establish an orange farm. The venture was moderately successful, but soon her father abandoned the family, disappearing and leaving them unsupported; a year later he was dead, having thrown himself from the prow of a ship in a Mexican harbour. Helen had been sent back to England, and it is not certain how much she knew of the rift between her parents or their financial difficulties; much of her later childhood was spent at boarding school.

When she was only nineteen she married Donald Ferguson, ten years her senior, and moved with him to colonial Burma where he was a railway administrator. The couple were ill matched, and their marital enmity would provide plenty of material for her later fiction. Not long after their son Bryan was born Helen returned with him to England, and the marriage was over. She studied painting in London, pursued her writing and travelled in continental Europe. While in France she met and began a love affair with Stuart Edmonds, the British artist who would eventually become her second husband. By this time she had already begun using heroin, an addiction that appears likely to have begun as a prescription of morphine for pain relief or depression.

For most of the 1930s the Edmonds lived quietly in the Chilterns, writing, painting and enjoying village life; Bryan visited in school holidays. Helen published six novels under her previous married name, Ferguson, garnering only moderate sales and reviews. During this period she also exhibited her paintings several times, and although she is little known as a visual artist she would continue to paint throughout her life. In 1935 she gave birth to a child who died soon after; the couple immediately adopted a daughter. Towards the end of the decade the marriage had soured, and Stuart had begun an affair. Severely depressed, Helen attempted suicide and was sent to recover at a private Swiss clinic. Soon after her return to England she met Ian Hamilton, a playwright who had been living for many years in New Zealand. They began a cautious affair, for he was still married and had plans to return to New Zealand, and she was still under the care of a psychiatrist. Helen's experience of depression and psychiatric treatment had inspired a collection of stories – much sparser, darker and more fantastic than her earlier writing – which would become *Asylum Piece* (1940), the first book she published as Anna Kavan. Not long after she had submitted the manuscript to her publisher, she and Hamilton left the country, travelling in Scandinavia and, after war was declared, crossing the Atlantic to New York. They journeyed down the East Coast of the United States to Mexico City and eventually settled in La Jolla, California, for seven months.

Ian Hamilton finally returned to New Zealand, and Helen set out towards Singapore *en route* to join her mother in South Africa. The American architect and patron of the arts Charles Fuller was travelling on the same boat, and when travel restrictions prevented them from reaching their destination they spent some months together in what was then the Dutch East Indies. Fuller returned to New York in November, and Helen joined him, enjoying the renown of her literary success with *Asylum Piece*, which had been published to critical acclaim in Britain. It was during this short spell in New York that she began using the name Anna Kavan in her personal life. Fuller introduced her to other writers and artists, but social excitement did not compensate for financial insecurity and deep depression, and she attempted suicide again.

Missing the emotional support that Ian Hamilton had given her, Kavan wrote asking to join him in New Zealand, and she arrived in the country early in 1941. She spent nearly two years there, living self-sufficiently with Hamilton in a quiet village; it was a peaceful interlude without heroin or emotional drama. But Hamilton was profoundly pacifist, and New Zealand had little tolerance or understanding for conscientious objectors at this time. As it became increasingly likely that he would be interned for refusing to fight, leaving Kavan alone and without a home, she attempted again to reach her mother in South Africa and sailed for England. During the journey, another ship in her convoy was torpedoed and sunk, but she arrived safely in January 1943 only to find that she was unable to obtain a travel permit and was to be conscripted for war work. She took a job at the Mill Hill Emergency Hospital, working with soldiers suffering from war neurosis, but left to become an assistant at the arts journal *Horizon*, writing literary reviews and publishing several stories and articles in the magazine.

During this time she was using cocaine and amphetamines and she settled into an almost unbroken twenty-five years of controlled heroin addiction. She began to be treated by Dr Karl Bluth, a German writer and psychiatrist whose anti-fascist writings had necessitated his flight from Nazi persecution in the 1930s. Their relationship would evolve into a deep friendship and intellectual bond; they would collaborate on writing projects and Bluth would prescribe Kavan's heroin for the next twenty years. It is not clear whether or not the two were lovers, but Bluth's wife certainly resented the amount of time they spent together.

By the end of the war Kavan had lost both her children; her son had enlisted as a paratrooper and was killed, and she was denied custody of her adoptive daughter owing to her perceived mental instability. Serious heart problems forced her to give up the job at *Horizon*. The stories she had published in magazines during the war were collected with some others in *I Am Lazarus* (1945), which was well received, but the critical failure of her most surrealist work, the novel *Sleep Has His House* (1947), made finding a publisher difficult for some years. She and Dr Bluth collaborated on an absurdist political satire, *The Horse's Tale* (1949), which was distributed only privately to friends after Bluth's money-saving scheme of having the book printed in Germany prevented its sale in the UK.

In 1950 Kavan's mother died, and, despite the immense wealth of her third husband, small provision had been made for Kavan in her will. The allowance that she had come to rely upon was cut drastically, and she felt disinherited, leaving her bitter towards the memory of her mother. To supplement her income she renovated several houses in West London and rented rooms to friends. She met the independent publisher Peter Owen, and he threw his support behind her writing, publishing her novel *Eagle's Nest* (1956) and a collection of stories *A Bright Green Field* (1958).

As both Kavan and the twentieth century moved into their seventh decade, she continued to take an interest in emerging culture and counterculture; her late writing shows the influences of mainstream film and television as well as contemporary avant-garde literature and science fiction. She revisited her early Helen Ferguson novel in which the character 'Anna Kavan' had first appeared, reworking a section of it into a shorter experimental narrative, *Who Are You?* (1963), but she was disappointed by its muted reception. Karl Bluth's death in 1964 precipitated another deep depression, but she found some respite from her grief in writing. Her dystopian novel *Ice* (1967) was her most successful book in two decades, but she had only a year to enjoy this late acclaim before she died of a heart attack in December 1968.

Kavan's writing is not to everyone's taste. Reading her work can be disorientating and discomforting; her narratives shift disconcertingly between past and present tense, first and third person. Her characters are often disagreeable, misanthropic, self-absorbed, priggish or delusional, and the paranoia of her nameless narrators is infectious. In one of her literary reviews she describes how the 'short story is like a small room in which is concentrated a brilliant light', and she found this form well suited to the intensity of her writing.

This current anthology draws together a selection of her stories from across nearly thirty years of writing, including the previously unpublished 'Starting a Career'. The extraordinary range of her style and the shifting 'environment and atmosphere' of the twentieth century are fully evident here: oblique portraits of crushing depression and incarceration from *Asylum Piece* (1940); moving evocations of wartime trauma from *I Am Lazarus* (1945); fantastic and surrealist pieces from *A Bright Green Field* (1958); and tales exploring altered states of consciousness from the posthumously published *Julia and the Bazooka* (1970). But each of these modes inflects the others: elements of science fiction begin to emerge at the beginning of the 1940s in 'Going Up in the World' and in her

1950s stories; the Blitz becomes surreal and hallucinatory in 'Our City'; and war continues to haunt the drug culture of late-1960s 'Julia and the Bazooka'.

As in all her writing, climatic atmosphere and emotional atmosphere suffuse these stories; extremes of heat and cold, gathering storms, enveloping fog and natural disaster provide the backdrop to intense human experience, and the boundary between inner and outer worlds becomes unstable. Her characters are often striving for, or mourning the loss of, love and understanding. Failed or thwarted connections are the raw substance of her writing: the memory or dream of a friend and lover in 'Asylum Piece II'; Kling's longing for communication with the dead in 'Face of My People'; the mute and languid bond of narrator and leopard in 'A Visit'. But there is also some playful, dark humour to be found in these tales, for Kavan loved absurdism, and the excessive horror in a story such as 'The Gannets' tips into misanthropic and hallucinatory bathos in 'The Old Address'. Several of the many unpublished manuscripts that accumulated during Kavan's lifetime have already been published posthumously; 'Starting a Career', a futuristic spy thriller undoubtedly influenced by James Bond, appears here for the first time. This story's wintry and futuristic setting, its tropes of genre fiction and its amoral protagonist who sets out to become the world's greatest enigma all recall her final novel *Ice*.

Kavan can only be described as a British writer, but she did not embrace her nationality. The periods of her life spent living in the United States, Burma and New Zealand, and her travels across Europe, Asia, South Africa and Mexico seem only to have emphasized her sense that, wherever she was in the world, she felt an outsider. Exile, homelessness and alienation are constant themes in her work. Her international outlook contributes to the difficulty in tracing her influences, because she read and experienced all sorts. As her *Horizon* reviews testify, she admired modernist writing, especially James Joyce, Virginia Woolf and T. S. Eliot; her work has been described as 'Kafkaesque', and she certainly considered Kafka to be one of the greatest writers. Her portraits of ill-fated and marginalized outsiders recall Jean Rhys, Jane Bowles, even Carson McCullers, and her experiments with surrealism beg comparison with other surrealist women writers such as Leonora Carrington, Unica Zürn and Ithell Colquhoun. There are shades of the weird fiction of H. P. Lovecraft in her work, and she draws on the rich legacy of gothic fiction, recalling stories by Isak Dinesen or Silvina Ocampo. Anaïs Nin, a great admirer of her work, observed parallels between their more experimental fiction, and her writing has some of the oblique intensity of Clarice Lispector. Her later work can also be compared with that of a younger generation of post-war British experimental writers, especially Ann Quin, Alan Burns and Muriel Spark. She was a fan of Brian Aldiss's writing and he of hers; J. G. Ballard and Doris Lessing both admired her, and their 'inner space fiction' recalls her work. She continued to engage with the work of continental European writers, including the Nouveau Roman; 'A Visit' undoubtedly engages with German writer Christoph Meckel's story 'The Lion'. These are only a handful of the multiple comparisons one can draw between Kavan's writing and that of other authors, and it is this diversity that makes her work so distinctive, rather than its isolation. Despite her relative obscurity, many authors today continue to draw inspiration from her.

In all the narrative about Kavan's life, little has been said about her politics, but political she most certainly was in her singular way. Her journalism, published in *Horizon* during the years 1943–6 demonstrates this plainly. The left–right political spectrum cannot accommodate her views any more than her fiction fits into conventional categories of literature; she was pacifist, nihilist, atheist, vehemently anti-fascist but without revolutionary vision – in fact, she rejected organized politics entirely and believed that collective society was inevitably totalitarian. Her ideals can be best described as individualist anarchist. Yet she believed in our mutual responsibility towards one another, and her focus on the individual was in part attentiveness to those who are dispossessed, marginalized and alone. Her pacifism during the Second World War did not extend as far as Ian Hamilton's, for she did not refuse to participate in war work, but she rejected any notion of heroism or glory, believing all parties to be guilty of terrible atrocities. Her conviction that human beings were hell-bent on their own destruction, and that of the natural world around them, is clearly evident in her writing during and after the war.

Kavan's life was not cut tragically short. She was sixty-seven when she died, and she had lived with various health problems, exacerbated by her heroin use, for much of her adult life. Her ashes were interred in her beloved garden in west London. It was only after her death that the mythology that has come to surround Anna Kavan began to accumulate, and she became, once again, a fiction. Tales of her heroin addiction, difficult temperament and enigmatic nature began to circulate in biographical pieces promoting her posthumous collections *Julia and the Bazooka* (1970) and *My Soul in China* (1975). She appeared as 'Karen' in a novel based on her marriage to Stuart Edmonds and, more recently, in a play about her friendship with Rhys Davies and in a French novel, *Anna K.** With no living relatives and limited archival sources, her characters' fictional experiences have been appropriated to enhance the known facts of her life. But if, as she believed, the truth of life can be found in fiction, it is fitting that her reality and her fantasy have become indistinguishable in the story of Anna Kavan.

VICTORIA WALKER

2019

---

*Rhys Davies's novel *Honeysuckle Girl* (London: Heinemann, 1975) was based on Kavan's marriage to Stuart Edmonds; D. J. Britton's play *Silverglass* (first performed at Swansea University, 13 September 2013) represents Kavan's friendship with Rhys Davies; Catherine LeNoble published a novel in French, *Anna K* (Orléans: Editions HYX, 2016).

MACHINES IN THE HEAD

GOING UP IN THE WORLD

IN THE LOW-LYING streets near the river where I live there is fog all through the winter. When I go to bed at night it is so cold that the pillow freezes my cheek. For a long time I have been lonely, cold and miserable. It is months since I have seen the sun. Suddenly, one morning, all this becomes intolerable to me. It seems that I can no longer bear the cold, the loneliness, the eternal fog – no, not even for another hour – and I decide to visit my Patrons and ask them to help me. It is a desperate resolve, but once I have made it I am filled with optimism. Perhaps I deliberately trick myself with false hopes as I put on my best dress and carefully make up my face.

At the last moment, just as I am ready to start, I remember that I ought to take a present with me. I have no money with which to buy a gift worthy of such great people: is there anything in the house that will do? In a panic I hurry from room to room, as if expecting to discover some valuable object, the existence of which I have over-looked all the time I've been living here. Of course there is nothing suitable. Some apples on the kitchen shelf catch my eye because even in this gloomy half-light their cheeks show up yellow and red. I hastily fetch a cloth and polish four of the yellowest apples until they shine. Then I line a small basket with fresh paper, arrange the apples inside and set out. On my way I tell myself that the simple fruit may please palates which have grown too accustomed to the flavour of hot-house peaches and grapes.

Soon I am in a lift, being whirled up towards the skies. A man-servant in white stockings and purple knee-breeches shows me into a magnificent room. Here one is above the fog, the sun is shining out-side the windows draped in soft veils of net, or, if it is not, it makes no difference, for the room is full of artificial sunshine from the con-cealed lights. The floor is covered by a carpet softer than moss, there are chairs and great sofas upholstered in delicate brocade, beautiful flowers are arranged in vases, some of which are shaped like shells and some like antique urns.

My Patrons are not present, and I am in no hurry to meet them. I am happy just to be in this warm room with its sunny, flower-scented air through which one almost expects to see butterflies flitting. After the foggy gloom to which I have grown accustomed it is like being transported to summer, to paradise.

Before very long my Patron appears. He is tall and fine-looking as such an important man ought to be. Everything about his appearance is perfect: his shoes gleam like chestnuts, his shirt is of finest silk, he wears a red carnation in his buttonhole and in his breast pocket is a handkerchief bearing a monogram embroidered by holy women. He greets me with charming courtesy, and we sit talking for a while on general topics. He addresses me as an equal. I begin to feel quite elated at such a promising start. Surely everything is going to turn out as I wish.

The door opens and my Patroness enters. We both rise to meet her. She is dressed in deep-blue velvet, and on her hat perches a small bird as vivid and rare as a jewel. There are pearls around her neck and diamonds on her smooth hands. She speaks to me with rather stilted brightness, smiling with narrow lips that do not unclose easily. Diffidently I offer my humble present, which is graciously accepted and then laid aside. My spirits fall somewhat. We sit down again in our cushioned seats and for a few minutes continue to maintain polite conversation. There comes a pause. I realize that the preliminaries are over and that it is time for me to state the object of my visit.

'I am freezing with cold and loneliness down there in the fog!' I exclaim in a voice that stammers with its own urgency. 'Please be kind to me. Let me share a little of your sunshine and warmth. I won't be any trouble to you.'

My companions glance at one another. A look of the deepest significance passes between them. I do not understand what the look means, but it makes me uneasy. It seems that they have already considered my petition and come to an understanding about it between themselves.

My Patron leans back in his chair and places the tips of his long fingers together. His cufflinks glitter; his hair shines like silk.

'We must treat this question objectively,' he begins. His voice has a reasonable, impartial sound, and I start to feel hopeful again. But as he goes on talking I perceive that the air of consideration which has impressed me so favourably is really nothing but a part of his perfect ensemble and no more to be relied upon than the flower in his buttonhole. In fact, he is not to be trusted.

'Don't think that I am accusing you,' he says, 'or setting myself up as your judge, but you must admit that your conduct towards us in the past has been far from satisfactory.'

He looks again at my Patroness who nods her head. The little bird in her hat seems to wink at me with its brilliant blind eyes.

'Yes,' says she, 'you have caused us a great deal of sorrow and anxiety by your bad behaviour. You have never consulted our wishes about anything but have obstinately gone your own way. It is only when you are in trouble that you come here asking us to look after you.'

'But you don't understand,' I cry, and I am ashamed to feel tears in my eyes. 'It's a matter of life and death this time. Please don't bring the past up against me now; I'm sorry if I've offended you; but you have everything, and you can afford to be generous. It can't mean very much to you. But, oh, if only you knew how I long to live in the sunshine again!'

My heart falls into my boots while I am speaking. I am plunged into despair because I see that neither of my hearers is capable of comprehending my appeal. I doubt if they are even listening to me. They do not know what fog is like; it is only a word to them. They do not know what it means to be sad and alone in a cold room where the sun never shines.

'We don't intend to be hard on you,' my Patron remarks, crossing his knees. 'No one will ever be able to say that we have not treated you with patience and forbearance. We will do our best to forget and forgive. But you, on your side, must promise to turn over a new leaf, to make a clean break with the past and give up your rebellious ways.'

His voice goes on, but now I am the one who is not listening. I have heard enough to fill me with hopeless disappointment. It is useless for me to attempt any further approach to people who are utterly inaccessible, utterly out of sympathy with me. Almost at my last gasp, I come to throw myself on their mercy, and a lecture is all they can find for me in their empty hearts. I sigh and undo my coat, which no one has invited me to remove and in which I am now uncomfortably warm. My eyes glance sadly about the handsome room, in the golden, flowery atmosphere of which butterflies might be floating. Through a glaze of tears I catch sight of my yellow apples pushed into a corner behind an enormous box of liqueur chocolates. I feel remorseful because I have brought them here only to be abandoned to indignity. Perhaps the valet or the chambermaid will take a bite out of one of them before they are thrown into the dustbin.

'You must set out with the fixed intention of doing your duty towards us,' my Patron is saying. 'You must try your hardest to wipe out past bad impressions. Above all you must demonstrate your gratitude towards your Patroness, earn her forgiveness and prove yourself worthy of her generosity.'

'And where am I to find a little warmth in all this?' I cry out desperately. What an incongruous sound the words have between these serene walls and how the fastidious flowers seem to toss their heads in disdain.

I know now that I have thrown away my last chance. There is no object in waiting a moment longer, so I get up and fly from the room. And at once the lift is swooping away with me, carrying me down to the cold, foggy streets where I belong.

THE ENEMY

SOMEWHERE IN THE WORLD I have an implacable enemy, although I do not know his name. I do not know what he looks like, either. In fact, if he were to walk into the room at this moment, while I am writing, I shouldn't be any the wiser. For a long time I believed that some instinct would warn me if we ever came face to face, but now I no longer think this is so. Perhaps he is a stranger to me; but much more probably he is someone whom I know quite well – perhaps someone I see every day. For if he is not a person in my immediate environment how does he come to possess such detailed information about my movements? It seems quite impossible for me to make any decision – even concerning such a trifling matter as visiting a friend for the evening – without my enemy knowing about it and taking steps to ensure my discomfiture. And, of course, as regards more important issues, he is just as well informed.

The fact that I know absolutely nothing about him makes life intolerable, for I am obliged to look upon everybody with equal suspicion. There is literally not a soul whom I can trust.

As the days go past I find that I am becoming more and more preoccupied with this wretched problem; indeed, it has become an obsession with me. Whenever I speak to anyone I catch myself scrutinizing him with secret attention, searching for some sign that would betray the traitor who is determined to ruin me. I cannot concentrate on my work because I am always debating in my mind the question of my enemy's identity and the cause of his hate. What act of mine can possibly have given rise to such a relentless persecution? I go over and over my past life without finding any clue. But perhaps the situation has arisen through no fault of my own but merely on account of some fortuitous circumstances that I know nothing about. Perhaps I am the victim of some mysterious political, religious or financial machination – some vast and shadowy plot, whose ramifications are so obscure as to appear to the uninitiated to be quite outside reason, requiring, for instance, something as apparently senseless as the destruction of everybody with red hair or with a mole on his left leg.

Because of this persecution my private life is already practically in ruins. My friends and family are alienated, my creative work is at a standstill, my manner has become nervous, gloomy and irritable, I am unsure of myself, even my voice has grown hesitating and indistinct.

You would think that my enemy might take pity on me now; that, seeing the miserable plight to which he has reduced me, he would be content with his vengeance and leave me in peace. But, no, I know perfectly well that he will never relent. He will never be satisfied until he has destroyed me utterly. It is the beginning of the end now, for during the last few weeks I have received almost certain indications that he is starting to lodge false accusations against me in official quarters. The time can't be far off when I shall be taken away. It will be at night, probably, that they will come for me. There will be no revolvers, no handcuffs; everything will be quiet and orderly with two or three men in uniform or white jackets, and one of them will carry a hypodermic syringe. That is how it will be with me. I know that I'm doomed, and I'm not going to struggle against my fate. I am only writing this down so that when you do not see me any more you will know that my enemy has finally triumphed.

AIRING A GRIEVANCE

YESTERDAY I WENT TO see my official adviser. I have visited him fairly often during the last three months in spite of the inconvenience and expense of these interviews. When one's affairs are in such a desperate state as mine, one is simply obliged to make use of any possible help, and this man D has been my last hope. He has been the only source of advice and assistance available to me, the only person with whom I could discuss my affairs: in fact, the only person to whom I could speak openly about the intolerable situation in which I have been placed. With everybody else I have had to be reserved and suspicious, remembering the motto 'Silence is a friend that never betrays anyone.' For how can I tell whether the person to whom I am talking is not an enemy or perhaps connected with my accusers or with those who will ultimately decide my fate?

Even with D I have always been on my guard. From the start there have been days when something seemed to warn me that he was not altogether to be trusted, yet on other occasions he filled me with confidence; and what was to become of me if I were deprived even of his support – unsatisfactory as it might be? No, I really couldn't face the future entirely alone, and so, for my own sake, I *must* not distrust him.

I went to him confidently enough in the first place. His name was known to me as that of a man, still young but already very near the top of his profession. I considered myself lucky to have been placed in his charge, notwithstanding the long journey which separated me from him: in those early days I did not anticipate having to visit him frequently. At the beginning I was favourably impressed by his solid town house and by the room in which he received me with its wine-coloured velvet curtains, its comfortable armchairs, its valuable-looking pieces of tapestry.

About the man himself I was not so certain. I have always believed that people of similar physical characteristics fall into corresponding mental groups, and he belonged to a type which I have constantly found unsympathetic. All the same, there could be no doubt as to his ability; he was excellently qualified to take charge of my case, and as I was only to meet him occasionally – and then in a professional and not in a social capacity – the fact of our being basically antipathetic to one another seemed of little significance. The main thing was that he should devote sufficient time to my affairs, that he should study my interests seriously, and this, to begin with, he seemed quite prepared to do.

It was only later, as things went from bad to worse and I was obliged to consult him at shorter and shorter intervals, that I started to feel dubious about his goodwill towards me.

At our early meetings he always treated me with extreme consideration, even with deference, listening with the closest attention to everything I had to say and in general impressing me with the grave importance of my case. Irrational as it may sound, it was this very attitude of his – originally so gratifying – which aroused my first vague suspicions. If he were really looking after my interests as thoroughly as he asserted, why was it necessary for him to behave in this almost propitiatory way which suggested either that he was trying to distract my attention from some possible negligence on his part or that matters were not progressing as favourably as he affirmed? Yet, as I have previously mentioned, he had a knack of inspiring confidence, and with a few encouraging, convincing phrases he could dispel all my tenuous doubts and fears.

But presently another cause for suspicion pricked my uneasy mind. Ever since my introduction to D, I had been aware of something dimly familiar about his face with the very black brows accentuating deep-set eyes into which I never looked long enough or directly enough to determine their colour but which I assumed to be dark brown. From time to time my thoughts idly pursued the half-remembered image which I could never quite manage to bring into full consciousness. Without ever really giving much attention to the subject, I think I finally decided that D must remind me of some portrait seen long before in a gallery, most probably somewhere abroad, for his coun-tenance was decidedly foreign and contained the curious balance of latent sensuality and dominant intellectualism seen to the best advantage in some of the work of El Greco. Then one day, just as I was leaving his house, the complete memory which had eluded me for so long suddenly came to me with an impact sharp as a collision with a fellow pedestrian. It was no ancient portrait that D's face recalled to my mind but a press photograph, and one that I had seen comparatively recently, one that was contained in an illustrated periodical which was probably still lying about somewhere in my living-room.

As soon as I got home I started to search through the papers which, in my preoccupied state of mind, I had allowed to accumulate in an untidy pile. It was not long before I found what I was looking for. The face of the young assassin, gazing darkly at me from the page, was, in all essentials, the same black-browed face that had confronted me a short time previously in the curtained seclusion of his handsome room.

Why did this accidental likeness make such an impression on me, I wonder? It is possible for a man to resemble a certain murderer in his outward appearance without possessing himself any violent ten-dencies; or if, as is more likely, he does possess them, without lacking sufficient restraint to hold them in check. One has only to think of D's responsible position, to look at his controlled, serene, intelligent face, to realize the fantastic nature of the comparison. The whole sequence of ideas is utterly grotesque, utterly illogical. And yet there it is; I can't banish it from my mind.

One must remember, too, that the man in the photograph was no common assassin but a fanatic, a man of extraordinarily strong convictions, who killed not for personal gain but for a principle, for what he considered to be the right. Is this an argument against D or in his favour? Sometimes I think one way, sometimes the other: I am quite unable to decide.

As a result of these prejudices – and, of course, there were others which would take too long to write down here – I decided to put my case in the hands of a different adviser. This was a serious step, not to be taken lightly, and I expended a great deal of time considering the subject before I finally sent off my application. Even after I had posted the letter I could not feel at all sure that I had done the right thing. Certainly, I had heard of people who changed their advisers, not once but several times, and of some who seemed to spend their whole time running from one to another, but I had always rather despised them for their instability, and the general feeling in the public mind was that the cases of these individuals would terminate badly. Still, on the whole, I felt that the exceptional circumstances warranted the change where I was concerned. In wording my letter of application I was particularly careful to avoid any statement that could possibly be taken as detrimental to D, merely stressing the point of how expensive and awkward it was for me to be continually undertaking the long journey to his house and asking for my case to be transferred to someone in the university town near my home.

For several days I waited anxiously for an answer, only to receive at the end of that time a bundle of complicated forms to be filled up in duplicate. These I completed, sent off and then waited again. How much of my life lately has consisted of this helpless, soul-destroying suspense! The waiting goes on and on, day after day, week after week, and yet one never gets used to it. Well, at last the reply came back on the usual stiff pale-blue paper, the very sight of which I have learned to dread. My request was refused. No explanation was given as to why a favour which had been granted to hundreds of people should be denied to me. But, of course, one can't expect explanations from these officials; their conduct is always completely autocratic and incalculable. All they condescended to add to the categorical negative was the statement that I was at liberty to dispense altogether with the services of an adviser should I prefer to do so.

I was so cast down after the receipt of this arbitrary communication that for two whole weeks I remained at home, absolutely inactive. I had not even the heart to go out of doors but stayed in my room, saying that I was ill and seeing no one except the servant who brought my meals. Indeed, the plea of illness was no untruth, for I felt utterly wretched in body as well as in mind, exhausted, listless and depressed as if after a severe fever.

Alone in my room, I pondered endlessly over the situation. Why, in heaven's name, had the authorities refused my application when I knew for a fact that other people were allowed to change their advisers at will? Did the refusal mean that there was some special aspect of my case which differentiated it from the others? If this were so, it must surely indicate that a more serious view was taken of mine than of the rest, as I was to be denied ordinary privileges. If only I knew – if only I could find out something definite! With extreme care I drafted another letter and sent it off to the official address, politely, I'm afraid even servilely, beseeching an answer to my questions. What a fool I was to humiliate myself so uselessly, most likely for the benefit of a roomful of junior clerks who doubtless had a good laugh over my laboriously thought-out composition before tossing it into the wastepaper basket! Naturally, no reply was forthcoming.

I waited a few days longer in a state of alternate agitation and despair that became hourly more unbearable. At last – yesterday – I reached a point where I could no longer endure so much tension. There was only one person in the whole world to whom I could unburden my mind, only one person who might conceivably be able to relieve my suspense, and that was D, who was still, when all was said, my official adviser.

On the spur of the moment I decided to go and see him again. I was in a condition in which to take action of some sort had become an urgent necessity. I put on my things and went out to catch the train.

The sun was shining, and I was astonished to see that during the period I had remained indoors, too preoccupied with my troubles even to look out of the window, the season seemed to have passed from winter to spring. When last I had looked objectively at the hills I had seen a Bruegel-like landscape of snow and sepia trees, but now the snow had vanished except for a narrow whiteness bordering the northern edge of the highest point of the wood. From the windows of the train I saw hares playing among the fine emerald-green lines of the winter wheat; the newly ploughed earth in the valleys looked rich as velvet. I opened the carriage window and felt the soft rush of air which, not far away, carried the plover in their strange, reeling love dance. When the train slowed down between high banks I saw the glossy yellow cups of celandines in the grass.

Even in the city there was a feeling of gladness, of renewed life. People walked briskly towards appointments or dawdled before the shop windows with contented faces. Some whistled or sang quietly to themselves under cover of the traffic's noise, some swung their arms, some thrust their hands deep in their pockets, others had already discarded their overcoats. Flowers were being sold at the street corners. Although the sunlight could not reach to the bottom of the deep streets the house-tops were brightly gilded, and many eyes were raised automatically to the burnished roofs and the soft, promising sky.

I, too, was influenced by the beneficent atmosphere of the day. As I walked along I determined to put the whole matter of the letter and its answer frankly before D, to conceal nothing from him but to ask him what he thought lay behind this new official move. After all, I had not done anything that should offend him; my request for a change of adviser was perfectly justifiable on practical grounds.

Nor had I any real reason for distrusting him. On the contrary, it was now more than ever essential that I should have implicit faith in him, since he alone was empowered to advance my cause. Surely, if only for the sake of his own high reputation, he would do everything possible to help me.

I reached his house and stood waiting for the door to be opened. A beggar was standing close to the area railings holding a tray of matches in front of him; a thin, youngish man of middle-class appearance, carefully shaved and wearing a very old, neat dark-blue suit. Of course, the whole town is full of destitute people, one sees them everywhere, but I couldn't help wishing that I had not caught sight, just at this moment, of this particular man who looked as though he might be a schoolmaster fallen on evil days. We were so close together that I expected him to beg from me; but instead of that he stood without even glancing in my direction, without even troubling to display his matches to the passers-by, an expression of complete apathy on his face that in an instant began to dissipate for me all the optimistic influence of the day.

As I went inside the door, some part of my attention remained fixed on the respectable-looking beggar with whom I seemed in some way to connect myself. The thought crossed my mind that perhaps one day I, no longer able to work, my small fortune absorbed in adviser's fees, my friends irreparably alienated, might be placed in the same situation as he.

The manservant informed me that D had been called out on urgent business but that he would be back before long. I was shown into a room and asked to wait. Alone here, all my depression, briefly banished by the sun, began to return. After the spring-like air outside, the room felt close and oppressive, but a sort of gloomy inertia prevented me from opening one of the thickly draped windows. An enormous grandfather clock in the corner didactically ticked the minutes away. Listening to that insistent ticking, a sense of abysmal futility gradually overwhelmed me. The fact of D's absence, that he should choose today of all days to keep me waiting in this dismal room, created the worst possible impression on my overwrought nerves. A feeling of despair, as if every effort I might make would inevitably be in vain, took possession of me. I sat lethargically on a straight-backed, uncomfortable chair with a leather seat, gazing indifferently at the clock, the hands of which had now completed a half-circle since my arrival. I thought of going away but lacked even the energy to move. An apathy, similar to that displayed by the beggar outside, had come over me. I felt convinced that already, before I had even spoken to D, the visit had been a failure.

Suddenly the servant returned to say that D was at my disposal. But now I no longer wanted to see him, it was only with the greatest difficulty that I forced myself to stand up and follow the man into the room where my adviser sat at his desk. I don't know why the sight of him sitting in his accustomed pose should have suggested to me the idea that he had not really been called out at all but had been sitting there the whole time, keeping me waiting for some ulterior motive of his own; perhaps to produce in me just such a sensation of despair as I now experienced.

We shook hands. I sat down and began to speak, driving my sluggish tongue to frame words that seemed useless even before they were uttered. Was it my fancy that D listened less attentively than on previous occasions, fidgeting with his fountain pen or with the papers in front of him? It was not long before something in his attitude convinced me that he was thoroughly acquainted with the whole story of my letter of application and its sequel. No doubt the authorities had referred the matter to him – with what bias, with what implication? And now my indifferent mood changed to one of suspicion and alarm as I tried to guess what this intercommunication portended.

I heard myself advancing the old argument of inconvenience, explaining in hesitant tones that in order to spend less than an hour with him I must be nearly six hours on the double journey. And then

I heard him answer that I should no longer have cause to complain of this tedious travelling, as he was just about to start on a holiday of indefinite length and would undertake no further work until his return.

If I felt despairing before you can imagine how this information affected me. Somehow I took leave of him, somehow found my way through the streets, somehow reached the train which carried me across the now sunless landscape.

How hard it is to sit at home with nothing to do but wait. To wait – the most difficult thing in the whole world. To wait – with no living soul in whom to confide one's doubts, one's fears, one's relentless hopes. To wait – not knowing whether D's words are to be construed into an official edict depriving me of all assistance or whether he intends to take up my case again in the distant future, or whether the case is already concluded. To wait – only to wait – without even the final merciful deprivation of hope.

Sometimes I think that some secret court must have tried and condemned me, unheard, to this heavy sentence.

THE SUMMONS

R IS ONE OF my oldest friends. Once, long ago, we used to live in flats in the same building, and then, of course, I saw a great deal of him. Afterwards the circumstances of our lives altered, wider and wider distances divided us, we could meet only rarely and with difficulty – perhaps only once or twice in a whole year – and then only for a few hours or at most for a weekend. In spite of this our friendship – which was purely platonic – continued unbroken, although it was naturally not possible to maintain quite the original degree of intimacy. I still felt that a close and indestructible understanding existed between R and myself: an understanding which had its roots in some fundamental character similarity and was therefore exempt from the accidents of change.

A particularly long interval had elapsed since our last encounter, so I was delighted when we were at length able to arrange a new meeting. It was settled that we should meet in town, have dinner together and travel by train later in the evening to the suburb where R was living.

Our appointment was for seven o'clock. I was the first to arrive at the restaurant, and, as soon as I had put my bag in the cloakroom, I went upstairs to the little bar which I often visited and where I felt quite at home. I noticed that a waiter was helping the usual barman, and, in the idle way in which one's thoughts run when one is waiting for somebody, I wondered why an assistant had been brought in that evening, for there were not many customers in the bar.

R appeared almost immediately. We greeted each other with

happiness and at once fell into a conversation which might have been broken off only the previous day.

We sat down and ordered our drinks. It was the waiter and not the barman who attended to us. As the man put down the two glasses on the table, I was struck by his ugliness. I know that one should not allow oneself to be too much influenced by appearances, but there was something in this fellow's aspect by which I couldn't help feeling repelled. The word 'troglodyte' came into my head as I looked at him. I don't know what the cave dwellers really looked like, but I feel that they ought to have been very much like this small, thick-set, colourless individual. Without being actually deformed in any way, he seemed curiously misshapen; perhaps it was just that he was badly proportioned and rather stooping. He was not an old man, but his face conveyed a queer impression of antiquity, of something hoary and almost obscene, like a survival of the primitive world. I remember particularly his wide, grey, unshaped lips which looked incapable of anything so civilized as a smile.

Extraordinary as it seems, I must have been paying more attention to the waiter than to my friend, for it was not until after we had lifted our glasses that I noticed a certain slight alteration in R's appearance. He had put on a little weight since our previous meeting and looked altogether more prosperous. He was wearing a new suit, too, and when I complimented him upon it he told me that he had bought it that day out of a considerable sum of money which he had received as an advance on his latest book.

I was very glad to hear that things were going so well with him. Yet at the same time a small arrow of jealously pierced my heart. My own affairs were in such a very bad way that it was impossible for me not to contrast my failure with his success, which seemed in some indefinable manner to render him less accessible to me, although his attitude was as friendly and charming as it had ever been.

When we had finished our drinks we went down to the restaurant for dinner. Here I was surprised and, I must admit, rather unreasonably annoyed to see the same waiter approaching us with the menu. 'What, are you working down here as well as upstairs?' I asked him, irritably enough. R must have been astonished by my disagreeable tone, for he looked sharply at me. The man answered quite politely that his work in the bar was finished for the evening and that he was now transferred to the restaurant. I would have suggested moving to a table served by a different waiter, but I felt too ashamed to do so. I was very mortified at having made such an irrational and unamiable display of feeling in front of R, who, I felt sure, must be criticizing me adversely.

It was a bad start to the meal. All on account of this confounded waiter, the evening had acquired an unfortunate tendency, like a run of bad luck at cards which one cannot break. Although we talked without any constraint, some essential spark, which on other occasions had always been struck from our mutual contact, now withheld from us its warmth. It even seemed to me that the food was not as good as usual.

I was glad when the waiter brushed away the crumbs with his napkin and set the coffee before us. Now at last we should be relieved of the burden of his inauspicious proximity. But in a few minutes he came back and, putting his repulsive face close to mine, informed me that I was wanted outside in the hall.

'But that's impossible – it must be a mistake. Nobody knows I'm here,' I protested, while he unemphatically and obstinately insisted that someone was asking for me.

R suggested that I had better go and investigate. So out I went to the hall where several people were sitting or standing about, waiting to meet their friends. I could see at a glance that they were all strangers to me. The waiter led me up to a man of late middle age, neatly and inconspicuously dressed, with a nondescript, roundish face and a small grey moustache. He might have been a bank manager or some such respectable citizen. I think he was bald-headed. He bowed and greeted me by my name.

'How do you know who I am?' I asked in amazement. I was positive that I had never seen him before, yet how could I be quite certain? His was one of those undistinguished faces which one might see many times without remembering it.

In reply, he began to reel off quite a long speech, but all so fast and in such a low voice that I could only catch a word here and there and these did not make sense. Totally unable to follow what he was saying, I only vaguely got the impression that he was asking me to accompany him somewhere. Suddenly I saw that the suitcase standing on the floor near his feet was my own.

'What are you doing with my bag? How did you get it . . . ? The attendant had no right to let you take it out of the cloakroom,' I said angrily, stretching down for the handle. But before I could reach it he picked up the bag himself with a deprecating smile and carried it out of the door.

I followed him, full of indignation and eager to reclaim my property. In the street, pedestrians came between us, and I was unable to catch up with him until he had turned the corner into a narrow alley full of parked cars. It occurred to me that the man was out of his mind. I couldn't believe he intended to steal the suitcase; he looked far too respectable for that.

'What's the meaning of all this? Where are you taking my bag?' I said, catching hold of his sleeve. We were just beside a large black limousine which stood in the rank of waiting cars. My companion rested the bag on the running board.

'I see that you haven't understood me,' he said; and now, for the first time, he spoke clearly so that I could really hear what he was saying. 'Here is my authorization. It was merely out of consideration for you that I refrained from producing it inside where everyone would have seen it.' He took a pale-blue form out of his pocket and held it towards me. But in the uncertain cross-light from the street lamps and the cars I only had time to make out some unintelligible legal phrases, and my own name embellished with elaborate scrolls and flourishes in the old-fashioned style, before he hastily put the stiff paper away again.

I was opening my mouth to ask him to let me look at it properly, when the chauffeur of the black car suddenly climbed out of the driving seat and picked up my case with the clear intention of putting it inside the vehicle.

'That belongs to me. Kindly leave it alone!' I commanded, at the same time wondering what I should do if the man refused to obey my order. But, as if the whole matter were of perfect indifference to him, he at once let go the handle and returned to his seat where he immediately appeared to become absorbed in an evening newspaper.

Now for the first time I observed the official coat of arms emblazoned on the glossy black door panel of the car, and I saw, too, that the windows were made of frosted glass. And for the first time I was aware of a faint anxiety, not because I thought for an instant that the situation was serious but because I had always heard what a tedious, interminable business it was to extricate oneself from official red tape once one had become even remotely involved with it.

Feeling that there was not a moment to be lost, that I must make my explanations and escape before I became any further entangled in this ridiculous mesh of misunderstanding, I began to talk to the elderly man who was standing patiently beside me. I spoke quietly and in a reasonable tone, telling him that I was not blaming him in the least but that a mistake had certainly been made; I was not the person mentioned on the document he had shown me, which probably referred to somebody of the same name. After all, my name was not an uncommon one; I could think of at least two people off-hand – a film actress and a writer of short stories – who were called by it. When I had finished speaking I looked at him anxiously to see how he had taken my arguments. He appeared to be impressed, nodded his head once or twice in a reflective way, but made no reply. Encouraged by his attitude, I decided on a bold move, picked up my suitcase and walked rapidly back to the restaurant. He did not attempt to stop me, nor, as far as I could see, was he following me, and I congratulated myself on having escaped so easily. It seemed as if boldness were what was most needed in dealing with officialdom.

R was still sitting at the table where I had left him. My spirits had now risen high. I felt cheerful, lively and full of confidence as I sat down – bringing my bag with me this time – and related the peculiar incidents that had just taken place. I told the story quite well, smiling at the absurdity of it; I really think I made it sound very amusing. But when, at the end, I looked for R's smile of appreciation, I was astonished to see that he remained grave. He did not look at me but sat with downcast eyes, drawing an invisible pattern on the cloth with his coffee spoon.

'Well – don't you think it was funny that they should make such a mistake?' I asked, trying to force his amusement.

Now indeed he looked up at me but with such a serious face and with eyes so troubled that all my assurance and good spirits suddenly evaporated into thin air. Just at that moment I noticed the ugly waiter hovering near, almost as if he were trying to overhear our conversation, and now a feeling of dread slowly distilled itself in my veins.

'Why don't you say something?' I burst out in agitation as R still remained silent. 'Surely it's not possible that you think – that there was no mistake . . . ? That I am the person they really wanted?'

My friend put down the spoon and laid his hand on my arm. The affectionate touch, so full of sympathy and compassion, demoralized me even more than his words.

'I think if I were you,' he said slowly and as if with difficulty, 'I think I would go and find out just what the charge is against you. After all, you will easily be able to prove your identity if there has really been a mistake. It will only create a bad impression if you refuse to go.'

Now that I have so much time on my hands in which to think over past events, I sometimes wonder whether R was right: whether

I would not have done better to keep my freedom as long as possible and even at the risk of prejudicing the final outcome of the affair. But at the time I allowed him to persuade me. I have always had a high opinion of his judgement, and I accepted it then. I felt, too, that I should forfeit his respect if I evaded the issue. But when we went out into the hall and I saw the neat, inconspicuous man still impassively, impersonally waiting, I began to wonder, as I have wondered ever since, whether the good opinion of anybody in the whole world is worth all that I have had to suffer and must still go on suffering – for how long; oh, for how long?

AT NIGHT

How slowly the minutes pass in the winter night, and yet the hours themselves do not seem so long. Already the church clock is calling the hour again in its dull country voice that sounds half stupefied with the cold. I lie in bed, and like a well-drilled prisoner, an old-timer, I resign myself to the familiar pattern of sleeplessness. It is a routine I know only too well.

My jailer is in the room with me, but he cannot accuse me of being rebellious or troublesome. I lie as still as if the bed were my coffin, not wishing to attract his attention. Perhaps if I don't move for a whole hour he will let me sleep.

Naturally, I cannot put on the light. The room is as dark as a box lined with black velvet that someone has dropped into a frozen well. Everything is quiet except when the house-bones creak in the frost or a lump of snow slides from the roof with a sound like a stealthy sigh. I open my eyes in the darkness. The eyelids feel stiff as if tears had congealed upon them in rime. If only I could see my jailer it would not be so bad. It would be a relief to know just where he is keeping watch. At first I fancy that he is standing like a dark curtain beside the door. The ceiling is lifted off the room as if it were the lid of a box, and he is towering up, taller than an elm tree, up towards the icy mountains of the moon. But then it seems to me that I have made a mistake and that he is crouching on the floor quite close to me.

An iron band has been clamped around my head, and just at this moment the jailer strikes the cold metal a ringing blow which sends needles of pain into my eye sockets. He is showing his disapproval of my inquiring thoughts; or perhaps he merely wishes to assert his authority over me. At any rate, I hastily shut my eyes again and lie motionless, hardly daring to breathe, under the bedclothes.

To occupy my mind I begin to run through the formulae which the foreign doctor taught me when I first came under suspicion. I repeat to myself that there is no such person as a *victim* of sleeplessness, that I stay awake simply because I prefer to continue my thoughts. I try to imagine myself in the skin of a newborn infant, without future or past. If the jailer looks into my mind now, I think, he cannot raise any objection to what is going on there. The face of the Dutch doctor, thin and sharp and hard like the face of a sea captain, passes before me. Suddenly a cock crows near by with a sound fantastic, unearthly, in this world still locked in darkness and frost. The cock's crow flowers sharply in three flaming points, a fiery fleur-de-lis blossoming momentaneously in the black field of night.

Now I am almost on the point of falling asleep. My body feels limp; my thoughts start to run together. My thoughts have become strands of weed, of no special colour, slowly undulating in colourless water.

My left hand twitches, and again I am wide awake. It is the striking of the church clock that has called me back to my jailer's presence. Did I count five strokes or four? I am too tired to be certain. In any case, the night will be over soon. The iron band on my head has tightened and slipped down so that it presses against my eyeballs. And yet the pain does not seem so much to come from this cruel pressure as to emanate from somewhere inside my skull, from the brain cortex: it is the brain itself which is aching.

All at once I feel desperate, outraged. Why am I alone doomed to spend nights of torment with an unseen jailer when all the rest of the world sleeps peacefully? By what laws have I been tried and condemned, without my knowledge, and to such a heavy sentence, too, when I do not even know of what or by whom I have been indicted? A wild impulse comes to me to protest, to demand a hearing, to refuse to submit any longer to such injustice.

But to whom can one appeal when one does not even know where to find the judge? How can one ever hope to prove one's innocence when there is no means of knowing of what one has been accused? No, there's no justice for people like us in the world: all that we can do is to suffer as bravely as possible and put our oppressors to shame.

MACHINES IN THE HEAD

THERE IS SOME QUITE trivial, distant noise; a sound, moreover, which has nothing to do with me, to which there is not the slightest need for me to pay any attention, yet it suffices to wake me and in no gentle way, either, but savagely, violently, shockingly, like an air-raid alarm. The clock is just striking seven. I have been asleep perhaps one hour, perhaps two. Roused in this brutal fashion, I jump up just in time to catch a glimpse of the vanishing hem of sleep as, like a dark scarf maliciously snatched away, it glides over the foot of the bed and disappears in a flash under the closed door. Useless, quite futile, to dash after it in pursuit. I am awake now for good or, rather, for bad; the wheels, my masters, are already vibrating with incipient motion; the whole mechanism is preparing to begin the monotonous, hateful functioning of which I am the dispirited slave.

'Stop! Wait a little – it's so early – Give me a little respite!' I cry, although I know it is quite in vain. 'Only let me have a little more sleep – an hour – half an hour – that's all I ask.'

What's the good of appealing to senseless machinery? The cogs are moving, the engines are slowly gathering momentum; a low humming noise is perceptible even now. How well I recognize every sound, every tremor of the laborious start. The loathsome familiarity of the routine is almost the worst part of it, intolerable and inescapable at the same time, like a sickness inside the blood. This morning it drives me to rebellion, to madness; I want to batter my head on the walls, to shatter my head with bullets, to beat the machines into pulp, into powder, along with my skull.

'It's horribly unjust!' I hear myself calling out – to what, to whom, heaven alone knows. 'One can't work so many hours on so little sleep. Doesn't anyone know or care that I'm dying here among all these levers and wheels? Can't somebody save me? I haven't really done anything wrong – I feel terribly ill – I can hardly open my eyes –'

And it's true that my head aches abominably, and I feel on the point of collapse.

Suddenly I notice that the light which hurts my eyes so much comes from the sun. Yes, the sun is actually shining outside; instead of snow there is dew sparkling all over the grass, crocuses have spread their neat, low fire of symmetrical flames under the rose bushes. Winter has gone; it is spring. In astonishment I hurry to the window and look out. What has happened, then? I feel dazed, bewildered. Is it possible that I am still living in a world where the sun shines and flowers appear in the springtime? I thought I had been exiled from all that long ago. I rub my tired eyes; still there is sunlight, the rooks flap noisily about their nests in the old elms, and now I hear how sweetly the small birds are singing. But even as I stand there all these happy things start to recede, to become phantasmal, transparent as the texture of dream plasma, banished by the monstrous mechanical outlines of pulleys, wheels, shafts, which in their orderly, remorseless and too-well-known evolutions now with increasing insistence demand my attention.

Like a fading mirage in the background I can still, straining my eyes, faintly discern the sunlit grass, the blue, blue arches of sky across which a green shape flies in remote parabola, the ghost of an emerald dagger spectrally flung.

'Oh, stop – stop! Give me another minute – just a minute longer to see the green woodpecker!' I implore, with my hands already, in automatic obedience, starting to perform their detested task.

What does a machine care about green woodpeckers? The wheels revolve faster, the pistons slide smoothly in their cylinders, the noise of machinery fills the whole world. Long since cowed into slavish submission, I still draw from some inexorable source the strength to continue my hard labour, although I am scarcely able to stand on my feet.

In a polished surface of metal I happen to notice my reflected face; it wears a pale, beaten, lonely look, eyes looking out at nothing with an expression of fear, frightened and lonely in a nightmare world. Something, I don't know what, makes me think of my childhood; I remember myself as a schoolchild sitting at a hard wooden desk, and then as a little girl with thick, fair, wind-tossed hair feeding the swans in a park. And it seems both strange and sad to me that all those childish years were spent in preparation for this – that, forgotten by everybody, with a beaten face, I should serve machinery in a place far away from the sun.

ASYLUM PIECE II

I HAD A FRIEND, a lover. Or did I dream it? So many dreams are crowding upon me now that I can scarcely tell true from false: dreams like light imprisoned in bright mineral caves; hot, heavy dreams; ice-age dreams; dreams like machines in the head. I lie between the bare wall and the medicine bitter with sediment in its dwarfish glass and try to recall my dream.

I see myself walking hand in hand with another, a human being whose heart and mind had grown into mine. We walked together on many roads, in sunshine beside ancient olive trees, on hillsides sprayed as by fountains with the larks' singing, in lanes where the raindrops dripped from the chilly leaves. Between us there was understanding without reservations and indestructible peace. I, who had been lonely and incomplete, was now fulfilled. Our thoughts ran together like greyhounds of equal swiftness. Perfection like music was in our united thoughts.

I remember an inn in some southern country. A crisis, long since forgotten, had arisen in our lives. I remember only the cypresses' black flames blowing, the sky hard as a blue plate, and my own confidence, serene, unshakeable, utterly secure. 'Whatever happens is trivial so long as we are together. Under no circumstances could we fail one another, wound one another, do one another wrong.'

Who shall describe the slow and lamentable cooling of the heart? On what day does one first observe the infinitesimal crack which finally becomes a chasm deeper than hell?

The years passed like the steps of a staircase leading lower and lower. I did not walk any more in the sun or hear the songs of larks like crystal fountains playing against the sky. No hand enfolded mine in the warm clasp of love. My thoughts were again solitary, disintegrant, disharmonious – the music gone. I lived alone in a few pleasant rooms, feeling my life run out aimlessly with the tedious hours: the life of an old maid ran out of my fingertips. I arranged the flowers in their vases.

Yet still, intermittently, I saw him, the companion whose heart and brain once seemed to have grown to mine. I saw him without seeing him, the same and yet not the same. Still I could not believe that everything was lost beyond hope of salvage. Still I believed that one day the world would change colour, a curtain would be ripped away, and all would be as it once was.

But now I am lying in a lonely bed. I am weak and confused. My muscles do not obey me, my thoughts run erratically, as small animals do when they are cornered. I am forgotten and lost.

It was he who brought me to this place. He took my hand. I almost heard the tearing of the curtain. For the first time in many months we rested together in peace.

Then they told me that he had gone. For a long while I did not believe it. But time passes by, and no word comes. I cannot deceive myself any longer. He has gone, he has left me, and he will not return. I am alone for ever in this room where the light burns all night long, and the professional faces of strangers, without warmth or pity, glance at me through the half-open door. I wait, I wait, between the wall and the bitter medicine in the glass. What am I waiting for? A screen of wrought iron covers the window; the house door is locked, although the door of my room is open. All night long the light watches me with its unbiased eye. There are strange sounds in the night. I wait, I wait, perhaps for the dreams that come so close to me now.

I had a friend, a lover. It was a dream.

THE END IN SIGHT

IT IS THREE DAYS since I received the official notification of my sentence; three days that have passed like shadows, like dreams.

The letter came through the post in the ordinary way and arrived by the afternoon delivery. Curiously enough, I was feeling more cheerful that afternoon than I had felt for a long time. The sun was shining, it was a lovely, calm day, one of those premature spring days which sometimes come to encourage us towards the end of a long, hard winter. The beautiful weather made me decide to go out; it really seemed shameful to stay shut up indoors with one's worries when the outside world was full of sunshine and life. I went across the fields towards the wood on the hill. This has always been a favourite walk of mine, and as I went I was astonished to think how long it was since I had last been that way and how my habits had changed, how I myself had altered, since the case started against me.

The colours of the landscape were as if washed pure and true in the transparent, windless light; vivid new sproutings like chilly flames appeared here and there in the hedges; the boughs of the trees were clouded with purplish buds. From the old yew on the hillside, disturbed by my footsteps, emerged with their strangely silent sure flight the two brown owls which I watched like old friends. Walking back to the house I made a resolution to go out more in future, not to stay indoors aimlessly brooding but to make the most of the natural world and to identify myself with non-human things, since they at least held no threat over me.

Oh, if only I'd known what I should find when I went inside

my door! But no premonition warned me of what was coming; on the contrary, as I've said, I felt more optimistic than I've felt since goodness knows when. I remember that as I crossed the garden from the field gate I was thinking about a man named David P whom I had met some time previously, a man who was in the same position as I was, waiting to hear the result of his case, and whose tranquil, courageous bearing under conditions of almost intolerable strain had aroused my admiration. 'How do you manage to keep so calm all the time?' I had asked him, half believing that he must be in possession of some inside information or perhaps had influence in official quarters. And I had remarked, too, on the fact that he alone of all the accused people I had ever met, wore an unanxious, almost happy expression.

'Oh, well, one doesn't gain anything by worrying, does one?' he had answered me. 'You may be sure that all the worrying in the world isn't going to affect the final issue for us. In fact, I'm inclined to believe that the less we think about our cases the better: if one has confidence in one's adviser one can safely leave everything to him. As for looking cheerful, there's still a lot left in life that we can enjoy. The great secret, in my opinion, is to concentrate on the things which can't be taken away from one – the past, for instance, and trees, and poetry . . .' Of course, I had often thought of this conversation before, but only now – and how ironic that realization should have come just then! – did I seem to realize the personal application of what David had said.

With these thoughts occupying my mind I went into the house. The afternoon post had come, and the letters were still lying on the floor where they had fallen when the postman pushed them through the slit in the door. I bent down to pick them up. At first there seemed to be nothing of interest, only a circular and one or two bills or receipts. But then, half hidden by a bulb catalogue, I saw the pale-blue official envelope; I felt the familiar stiffness of the paper in my hand, and my heart quickened its beat.

Right up to that moment I had no suspicion of what the letter contained. From time to time, ever since my case started, these pale-blue documents have descended upon me, sometimes with a form to be filled in, sometimes with an ambiguous message or with an extract from some incomprehensible blue book, and I, unsuspectingly, took this for another communication of the same kind. Even when I had torn open the envelope and read through the paper enclosed I failed at the start to take in the meaning of the words.

It can't be true – someone's playing a joke on me, I thought, as the import of the sentences slowly penetrated my mind. Surely this isn't how it's done – through the post – in this casual way . . . ? Surely they'd at least send somebody – a messenger . . . But then a curious vibration, like running water, seemed to flow over the walls. I saw the walls leaning nearer, as if watchfully. I knew very well that the letter was not a trick, and I was glad that I was alone in the hall with only the walls watching to see my face.

That was what happened three days ago. Since then time has passed in an unreal flux. Perhaps today, perhaps tomorrow, the final blow will fall; I know that I have, at the most, another week or ten days. What is the correct behaviour for a condemned person? – the authorities have never sent me a pamphlet containing that information! Sometimes I feel almost relieved to think that it is all over, that the suspense is finished at last. At other times it seems to me that I am quite incapable of realizing that this is the end. I look at the elm trees over which the thickening buds have flung a soft purple bloom, and it seems incredible that I shall not even see the leaves as big as the ears of mice. No, no – it's simply absurd – it can't be true . . . It's somebody else who has received the fatal pale-blue notification – perhaps David P. He would know how to behave in such circumstances; he would bear philosophically and with fortitude the sentence I am not brave enough even to contemplate.

I am constantly aware of the heart beating inside my breast, strongly and resolutely pumping the blood through my veins. Once

I read somewhere that when the blood is thin it wants to return whence it came. But my blood is not thin; my blood does not want to fall back. Unbearable reluctance of the blood that will not fall! How many, dying on the scaffold, must have suffered this unspeakable punishment, not to be justified by any penal code.

Yesterday afternoon I lay down on the couch in my living-room. I had scarcely slept at all the previous night, and I felt I must rest a little. But I had hardly put my head on the cushions when a voice seemed to shout in my ear, 'What, are you going to waste an hour with your eyes closed when perhaps this is their last hour for seeing anything?'

I jumped up, and like a demented person, like someone driven by furies, I hurried through the rooms of the house, hurried into the garden and into the fields, straining my eyes to appreciate every detail, straining to store up within my brain the images of all these things which are so soon to be hidden from me for ever. Later on, quite exhausted, I went into the inn for a drink, but no sooner was the glass in my hand than I felt an impulse to throw it away, unwilling to dim even with a single drop of alcohol the sharp vision of what might be the last scene upon which I should ever look.

People were there whom I knew. They laughed and spoke together about the coming summer and what they would do in the long summer days. How could I stay and listen to their talk, knowing that while they are carrying out the plans made so carelessly I shall be far from every activity? And how can I stay at home, either, answering the questions of the gardener about seeds for the summer and hearing the chatter of my little girl who knows nothing of what is happening to me and who also talks of the future, of the summer, and of what we will do together?

The hours pass, some slowly, some like flashes of light, but each one leading me inexorably nearer to the end. Incredulous, I watch the hours pass without bringing any reprieve. 'Isn't anyone going to do anything, then?' I want to cry out. 'Isn't anything going to happen to save me? They can't let me be destroyed like this. A message must come to say it was all a mistake. Somebody must do something.'

But no one around me even knows what is going on. Only the dog seems to sense that all is not well with me. And when, just now, unable to bear my sufferings any longer in silence, I whispered to him, 'Oh, Tige, I'll soon have to leave you – this dreadful thing is really going to happen to me – nothing will save me now,' I saw a dimness like tears in his lustrous brown eyes.

THERE IS NO END

'Whither shall I go from thy spirit? or whither shall I flee from thy
   presence?
If I ascend up into heaven, thou art there: if I make my bed in hell,
   behold, thou art there.
If I take the wings of the morning, and dwell in the uttermost parts
   of the sea;
Even there shall thy hand lead me.'

I CAN'T THINK PROPERLY these days, I find it difficult to remember,
but I suppose those words were written about Jehovah, although
they apply just as well to my enemy – if that is what I should call him.

'If I make my bed in hell, behold, thou art there.' That particular
phrase rings in my brain with a horrid aptness, for certainly I have
made my bed in hell, and certainly he is here with me. He is near
all the time, although I do not see him. Only sometimes, very early
in the morning before it has got light, I seem to catch a glimpse of a
half-familiar face peering in at the window; but it is always snatched
away so quickly that I have no time to recognize it. And just once,
one evening, the door of my room was suddenly opened a little way
and somebody glanced in through the crack, glanced in, and then
passed hurriedly out of sight down the corridor. Perhaps that was he.

Why does he keep his eye on me like this now that he has accom-
plished his purpose and brought about my destruction? It can't be to
make sure that I don't escape; oh no, there's no possibility of that, he
need not have the slightest fear. Is it just to gloat over my ruin? But,

no, I don't think that's the reason, either, for if that were so he would come more often and at times more humiliating to me when I am in the deepest despair.

Somehow I have the impression from those vague glimpses I have caught of his face that it wears a look that is not vindictive but kindred, almost as though he were related closely to me by some similarity of brain or blood. And of late the idea has come to me – fantastic enough, I admit – that possibly after all he is not my personal enemy but a sort of projection of myself, an identification of myself with the cruelty and destructiveness of the world. On a planet where there is so much natural conflict may there not very well exist in certain individuals an overwhelming affinity with frustration and death? And may this not result in an actual materialization, a sort of eidolon moving about the world?

I have thought a lot about such matters of late, sitting here and looking out of the window. For, strangely enough, there are windows without bars in this place and doors which are not even locked. Apparently there is nothing to prevent me from walking out whenever I feel inclined. Yet, although there is no visible barrier, I know only too well that I am surrounded by unseen and impassable walls which tower into the highest domes of the zenith and sink many miles below the surface of the earth.

So it has come upon me, the doom too long awaited, the end without end, the bannerless triumph of the enemy who, after all, appears to be close as a brother. Already it seems to me that I have spent a lifetime in this narrow room whose walls will continue to regard me with secrecy through innumerable lifetimes to come. Is it life, then, or death, stretching like an uncoloured stream behind and in front of me? There is no love here, nor hate, nor any point where feeling accumulates. In this nameless place nothing appears animate, nothing is close, nothing is real; I am pursued by the remembered scent of dust sprinkled with summer rain.

Outside my window there is a garden where nobody ever walks, a garden without seasons, for the trees are all evergreens. At certain times of the day I can hear the clatter of footsteps on the concrete covered ways which intersect the lawns, but the garden is always deserted, set for the casual appreciation of strangers, or else for the remote and solitary contemplation of eyes defeated like mine. In this impersonal garden, all neatness and vacancy, there is no arbour where friends could linger but only concrete paths along which people walk hurriedly, inattentive to the singing of birds.

PALACE OF SLEEP

THE WIND WAS BLOWING like mad in the hospital garden. It seemed to know that it was near a mental hospital and was showing off some crazy tricks of its own, pouncing first one way and then another and then apparently in all directions at once. The mad wind sprang out with a bellow from behind a corner of the nurses' quarters, immediately tearing around the back of the building to meet itself halfway along the front in a double blast that nearly snatched the cap from the head of a sister hurrying towards the entrance. With a clash and a clatter the door swung to admit her indignant figure huddled in its blue cloak. The wind came in, too, with a malicious gusto that died drearily in the recesses of the hall where the two doctors were talking.

The physician in charge glanced around as if he resented the unceremonious way the wind burst into his hospital. He was a man of about sixty-five, with a red cheerful face and white hair. Magnanimously passing over the wind's interruption, he went on with the story he was telling.

'When I went in next morning she was trying to tear up the sheet. So I said to her in a quiet, friendly way, "Don't you think that's rather a silly thing to do?" And she answered me back as quick as lightning, "If I can't do silly things here, I'd like to know where I can do them."' The red face creased into a net of jovial lines; the broad shoulders shook with laughter. 'Pretty smart, wasn't it?'

The young doctor echoed the laugh politely. He was a visitor from the north who was being shown around the hospital. Himself a reticent man, he wished that the superintendent were a little less genial and expansive. So much good humour aroused in him some disquietude, some slight distrust. He turned his lean, sensitive face, and his eyes rested reflectively on the other for a moment. What they saw was not altogether reassuring. There was something which they found faintly suspect about the appearance of the elderly man. His hair was too white, his face was too genial, his expression was too optimistic. He looked more like a country parson than a psychiatrist.

The visitor looked at his watch and said tentatively, 'I'm afraid I haven't much time left. I think you were going to show me the paying block – ?'

'Yes, yes. The paying block. You must certainly see that before you go. We're very proud of our private wards.'

The swing doors clashed behind the two men, who lowered their heads against the attack of the wind. The wind leaped madly upon them, with malice, with joy, as they walked on the covered way that crossed the impersonal garden. In the empty flower beds the earth lay saturated and black, the wintry looking acid-green grass rippled under the wind, the bare trees lashed their branches complainingly.

The two doctors walked briskly along side by side, the one tall, contemplative, reserved, turned in upon himself against the onslaught of wind, the other with white hair blowing about and a look of determined good nature which seemed to set the seal of his approval upon the rough weather.

The long brick building felt quiet as a vacuum after the windy tumult outside. The superintendent paused for a moment inside the door, smoothing his beautiful white hair with his fingers. He was slightly breathless.

'Welcome to the palace of sleep,' he said with his cheerful smile, speaking and smiling partly for the benefit of a young nurse who was passing by. 'All the patients in this wing are having partial or prolonged narcosis,' he went on in a more confidential tone as the girl disappeared through one of the many doors.

The wide corridor was coldly and antiseptically white, with a row of doors on the left and windows on the opposite side. The windows were high and barred and admitted a discouraging light that gleamed bluishly on the white distemper like a reflection of snow. Some grey rubber composition which deadened sound covered the floor. A handrail ran along the wall under the high windows.

One of the doors further down the corridor opened, and a nurse emerged, supporting a woman in a red dressing-gown. The patient swayed and staggered in spite of the firm grip that guided her hand to the rail. Her head swung loosely from side to side, her wide-open eyes, at once distracted and dull like the eyes of a drunken person, stared out of her pale face, curiously puffy and smooth under dark hair projecting in harsh, disorderly elf-locks. Her feet, clumsy and uncontrolled in their woollen slippers, tripped over the hem of her long nightdress and threw her entire weight on the nurse's supporting arm.

'Hold up, Topsy,' the probationer said in a tolerant, indifferent voice just perceptibly tinged with impatience, speaking as if to an awkward child. She hoisted her companion upright, and the pair continued their laborious progress towards the bathroom, the sick woman stumbling and reeling and gazing desperately, blankly ahead, the nurse watchful, abstracted and humming a dance tune under her breath.

'That patient will finish her treatment in another day or two,' the physician-in-charge told the visitor. 'Of course, she won't remember anything that's happened to her during the period of narcosis. She's practically unconscious now, although she can manage to walk after a fashion.'

He continued to discuss technicalities as they moved together along the corridor. The young man listened and answered somewhat mechanically, his eyes troubled, disturbed by what they had seen.

A door opened as the two doctors were passing it, and the red-faced senior paused to speak to the nurse who was coming out, holding an enamel tray covered with a cloth from beneath which emanated the nauseous stench of paraldehyde. He noticed the other man's instinctive recoil, and his face wrinkled into its jolly folds.

'Don't you like our local perfume, then? We're so used to the smell of PR here that we hardly notice it. Some of the patients say they actually get to like it in time.'

They went into the room, which was heavy with the same sickening odour. Under the white bedspread pulled straight and symmetrical, like the covering of a bier, a young woman was lying quite motionless with closed eyes. Her fair hair was spread on the pillow; her pale face was absolutely lifeless, void, with the peculiar glazed smoothness and eye sockets darkly circled. The superintendent stood at the bedside looking down at this shape which already seemed to have forfeited humanity and given itself over prematurely to death. His face wore a complacent expression, gratified, approving; the look of a man well satisfied with his work.

'She won't move now for eight hours, and then she'll come round enough to be washed and fed, and then we'll send her off for another eight-hour snooze.'

The visitor had come close to the bed and was also looking down at its occupant. The vague distress accumulating in his mind crystallized for some reason about this inanimate form which seemed, to his stimulated sensibilities, to be surrounded by an aura of inexpressible suffering.

'I don't know that I altogether approve of such drastic treatment for psycho-neurotics,' he was beginning, when suddenly a tremor disturbed the immobility of the anonymous face, the eyelids quivered under their load of shadows. The man watched, fascinated, almost appalled, as, slowly, with intolerable, incalculable effort, the drugged eyes opened and stared straight into his. Was it imagination, or did he perceive in their clouded greyness a look of terror, of wild supplication, of frantic, abysmal appeal?

'She's not conscious, of course,' the superintendent remarked in his benevolent voice. 'That opening of the eyes is purely a reflex. She can't really see us or hear anything we say.'

Smiling, white-headed like a clergyman, he turned and walked across to the open door. The other doctor hesitated for a few seconds in the ill-smelling room, looking down at the patient, held by an obscure reluctance to withdraw his gaze from those unclear eyes. And when he finally moved away he felt uneasy and almost ashamed and wished that he had not come to visit the hospital.

THE BLACKOUT

'I CAN'T REMEMBER ANYTHING that happened,' the boy said. 'It was like a blackout, sort of.'

He twisted his thin body uneasily on the couch where he was lying, and for a second his face, which seemed much too startled and meek and vulnerable for a soldier's face, was turned up towards the doctor sitting beside him; then he looked very quickly away.

Queer sort of looking bloke for a doctor, he thought, noticing transiently beside his shoulders the crossed legs in shabby grey trousers, the worn brogues with mended soles. He wished that the doctor were not there. The doctor's presence made him uneasy, although there was nothing to cause uneasiness about the look of the man.

The couch was comfortable. If he had been alone in the room the boy would have quite enjoyed lying there with a pillow under his head. The room was small and there was nothing at all alarming about it. The walls were pale green, enclosing no furniture but the couch, the chair on which the doctor sat and a desk. There was a calendar with a bright picture hanging over the desk. The boy could not see what was in the picture because, in order to look at it properly, he would have had to turn his head around in the doctor's direction. The sun was shining outside the window, which was open a bit at the top. The glass panes had been broken in a raid and replaced by an opaque plastic substance so that you couldn't see out. The boy wondered what was outside the window. He thought he would like, vaguely, to get up, open the bottom half of the window and have a

47

look and also to examine the picture on the calendar. The presence
of the doctor prohibited him from doing these things, so he looked
down at his hospital tie and began fidgeting with the loose ends of
it. The tie had been washed so often that it had faded from red to
deep pink and the cotton fabric had a curious dusty pile on it, almost
like velvet, which communicated an agreeable sensation to the tips
of his fingers.

'Which is the last day you can remember clearly?' the doctor asked.

'The day I was due to rejoin my unit,' the boy said, reluctantly
detaching a fragment of his attention from the pleasant feel of the tie.

'Do you remember what date it was?'

'September the eleventh.' He wasn't likely to forget that date,
so hypnotically, fascinated with dread, he had watched it racing
towards him through the telescoped days of his embarkation leave.

'Do you know what the date is today?'

He shook his head, looking down at the tie, and his very fine, limp
hair fluffed on the pillow where it was longest on the top of his head.

'It's the eighteenth. You started remembering things when you
were brought in here yesterday, so that means your blackout lasted
five complete days, doesn't it?'

'Yes, I suppose so,' the boy said and waited, in apprehension, for
the bad part to begin.

Why can't they leave you alone? he was thinking. Why must they
go on poking and prodding at you when all you wanted was to be left
in peace? It wasn't as if you would ever be able to tell them what they
wanted to know or as if they'd ever understand if you did. His fingers,
pleating the ends of the tie, gripped more abruptly the softness from
which they no longer derived any satisfaction.

'You remember everything that happened while you were on leave
quite distinctly?' the doctor asked him.

'Yes, oh yes,' the boy said at once, speaking fast, as if he hoped, by
bringing the words out quickly, in some way to terminate the matter
without touching on what was most painful.

'And where did you spend this leave?'

There now, it's begun now, the bad part's beginning, he thought in himself. And recognizing helplessly the preliminary movement of that thing which from the outset had filled him with a profound unease, he remained silent now while his mind ran from side to side, seeking the unknown avenues of defence or escape.

'Well, where did you spend your leave?'

The doctor's voice was casual and almost friendly, but there was much firmness in it, and also there came along with it the dangerous thing preparing to launch its attack, which could not be trifled with.

'I went home to my auntie,' the boy said, whispering.

Like looking back down a long tunnel he began remembering now that tenement place off the Wandsworth Road, the water tap out on the landing and the room always chock-a-block with the washing and cooking and the dirty dishes and pots that his mum never could keep upsides with, what with her heart, and his dad coming in drunk as often as not and knocking her about till the neighbours started opening their doors and threatening to call a policeman, and himself feeling shaky and sick and trying not to make a noise with his crying as he hid there crouched up in a ball of misery under the table. His auntie used to come visiting sometimes when his dad was away, and she was not old at all, or frightening or frightened at all, but so pretty and young and gay that maybe that was the reason he always thought the word auntie was a word you used as a kind of endearment, in the way sweetie and honey were used. When he was eight years old his dad got TB and gave up the drink, but it was too late then, his mum was dying already, and when his dad died later on in the san he felt only happier than he had ever been in his life because he was going to live with his auntie for ever and ever and there would be no more shouts or rows or crying or staring neighbours.

He remembered the little dark house where the two of them lived then in Bracken's Court – tiny and old-fashioned and a bit incon-venient it was with those steep stairs with a kink in them where his dad would surely have broken his neck if he'd ever come there after closing time – but cosy, too, like a dolls' house, and they'd always been happy in it together, even after the arthritis stopped his auntie from going out to her dress-making. When he left school he'd been taken on as messenger at the stationer's and later had got a salesman's job inside the shop and worked hard and was getting along well, so that it hadn't seemed to matter too much that she could do less and less of the work they sent her at home, because he was earning almost enough to take care of them both and soon it would be more than enough the way things were going. Then the war had come, and she had got worse, she had those bad headaches often and couldn't manage the crooked stairs. Then he had been called up, and he had hated it all, hated the army, hated leaving home, hated losing his good job, hated the idea of being sent overseas to fight, but most of all hated leaving her badly off now, financially insecure, bombs falling perhaps, and she alone with her crippling pains and no one reliable to take care of her; she who had always been sweet and lovely to him and deserved taking care of more than anyone in the world. When he thought of what might become of her if he were taken prisoner or killed it was more than he could bear, and he almost wished she were safely out of it all. Yes, when she went down with flu or whatever it was during his last leave, he almost hoped she wouldn't get well, it broke his heart so to leave her like that. But these were some of the things which never could be explained, and he wished only to be left alone and not be made to remember.

But the questions had to go on.

'What are the last things you remember doing before you left your aunt's house that final day?' the doctor wanted to know.

'I spent a goodish time straightening up and cleaning the place so as to leave everything shipshape,' the boy said. 'My auntie being an invalid more or less I wanted to leave things as easy for her as I could.'

Out of the end of his left eye he could see the doctor's crossed knees and the feet in their mended shoes, and for an instant rebellion rose in him because this was a man no different from himself who by no divine right of class or wealth or any accepted magic sought to force memory on him. But there was something beyond that: beyond just the man who could be opposed with obstinacy there was the frightening thing which he had to fight in the dark, and he knew that he dared not remain silent because his silence might be to that thing's advantage, and he went on, speaking low and mumbling as if the words came out against their will.

'We had tea about four. Then I went up and packed my kit. Then it was time to go for the train. I said goodbye and started for the station. King's Cross I had to go from.'

There was a long pause, and at the end of it came the doctor's voice asking if that was the last thing he could remember, and the boy's voice telling him that it was, and then there was silence again.

'That's queer,' the boy said suddenly into this silence. And now his voice sounded changed, there was astonishment and dismay in it, and the doctor uncrossed his knees and looked at him more closely, asking him, 'What's queer?'

'I've just remembered something,' the boy said. 'That time I told you about when I left the house, it wasn't the last time, really.'

'Not the last time you were in the house?'

'No. I've just remembered. It's just sort of come back to me somehow. When I'd gone part of the way to the station I found I'd left something important behind, my pay-book I think it was, and I had to sprint back to fetch it.'

The doctor took a packet of cigarettes out of his pocket and lighted one with his utility lighter, which never worked the first time he thumbed it, and blew out a little smoke. He seemed in no hurry at all about asking the next question.

'Can you remember how you were feeling when you went back?'

'I suppose I felt a bit flustered like anyone would about leaving my pay-book,' the boy said, defensive suddenly and blindly suspicious of some unimagined trap.

Looking into the tunnel he remembered fumbling under the mat for the key which was left there for the next-door woman who came in to give a hand. Was it as he came in or as he was going out again that he stood at the foot of the stairs where they crooked in the angle of a dog's hind leg out of the living-room? It was dusk, and he remembered the silence inside the house as though there were a dead person or somebody sleeping upstairs. Yes, she must have been asleep then, he thought, but whether he went up to her was not in the memory but only the noise of his army boots clattering away on the paving-stones of the court, and as he came out into the high street a church bell was ringing.

The doctor asked, 'What happened afterwards?'

'I can't remember anything more,' the boy said.

'Nothing whatever? Not even some isolated detail?'

'Yes,' he said, after a while. 'I think I remember looking for the station entrance, and a big bridge with a train shunting on it up high.'

He was aware, just then, of danger skirmishing all about in the green-walled room, and lying there on the couch his eyes were still down where they seemed safe on the pink ends of the tie, his hands clenched now and his neck and shoulders gone tense; and he not knowing if it were through his words or his silence that the danger would strike.

Why did a church bell keep ringing in the tunnel like that? It was a very deep tunnel into which he was being forced. He did not want to go down in the tunnel again. He was afraid. But because of the unknown thing whose immediate agent was the casual, near-friendly voice, nothing could save him from that black exploration split by the doleful and ugly clang of a distant bell.

'As if someone had died,' he said out loud.

'Who do you think might have died?'

No, no. Not that. Don't let it come, the boy thought, fighting desperately against what had all the time been waiting there behind every word; the worst thing, the intolerable pain, the fear not to be borne. And at once his nerves started to twitch and tears sprang in his eyes in case she might not have been sleeping but dead in the silent room at the top of the steep stairs, investigated or not by him he was, agonizingly, somehow unable to know.

Running in panic along the tunnel he remembered the alleyway, like something in a film he'd seen once, blank walls leaning nearer and nearer to suffocation, and, at the bend, a lamp-bracket sticking out with a dangling noose; only no corpse was at the end of the rope. And always the hurrying army boots and the bell ringing, till he did not know if it was the noise of his own steps or the church bell clanging inside his head. The noise was part of his hunger, and he remembered, further along the tunnel, scrounging about at night where a street market had been and finding, finally, in the gutter, a piece of sausage, grey, slimy, like the wrist of a dead baby, and the terrible thirst that came on him afterwards, and how he drank out of a horse-trough, scooping the water up with his hands, and it seemed all wrong because they killed animals painlessly. Then there was that open space; a heath or a common, where he had vomited and lain on the ground, his hair in the rough grass. He felt weak and stiff from the vomiting and clouds of insects were around him, settling on his face and hands and crawling over his mouth because he was too weak to flap at them, but in the end it got dark and the insects went away then and left him in peace.

Faster and faster he ran to escape from the tunnel and the tolling noise of the bell. And at last he was outside, the tunnel was getting smaller and smaller until it vanished, and there was respite from the tolling, nothing left now but the room with the doctor quietly smoking, sunshine outside the window, the calendar on the wall.

The boy was not lying on the couch any more but bending over with hunched shoulders as if hiding from something, his head on his raised knees in the posture a person might take crouching under a table, and although he was crying he was no longer thinking of the tunnel or of the dangerous secret thing which had scared him so terribly or about anything he could have put into any words.

'It was like a blackout. A blackout. I can't remember,' he kept on hopelessly mumbling among the tears.

FACE OF MY PEOPLE

BEFORE THEY TOOK OVER the big house and turned it into a psychiatric hospital the room must have been somebody's boudoir. It was upstairs, quite a small room, with a painted ceiling of cupids and flowers and doves, the walls divided by plaster mouldings to simulate pillars and wreaths, and the panels between the mouldings sky blue. It was a frivolous little room. The name Dr Pope looked like a mistake on the door and so did the furniture, which was not at all frivolous but ugly and utilitarian, the big office desk, the rather ominous high hard thing that was neither a bed nor a couch.

Dr Pope did not look at all frivolous either. He was about forty, tall, straight, muscular, with a large, impersonal, hairless, tidy face, rather alarmingly alert and determined-looking. He did not look in the least like a holy father or, for that matter, like any sort of a father. If one thought of him in terms of the family he was more like an efficient and intolerant elder brother who would have no patience with the weaknesses of younger siblings.

Dr Pope came into his room after lunch, walking fast as he always did, and shut the door after him. He did not look at the painted ceiling or out of the open window through which came sunshine and the pleasant rustle of trees. Although the day was warm he wore a thick, dark double-breasted suit and did not seem hot in it. He sat down at once at the desk.

There was a pile of coloured folders in front of him. He took the top folder from the pile and opened it and began reading the typed case notes inside. He read carefully, with the easy concentration of an untroubled single-mindedness. Occasionally, if any point required consideration, he looked up from the page and stared reflectively at the blue wall over the desk where he had fastened with drawing pins a number of tables and charts. These pauses for reflection never lasted more than a few seconds; he made his decisions quickly, and they were final. He went on steadily reading, holding his fountain pen and sometimes making a note on the typescript in firm, small, legible handwriting.

Presently there was a knock, and he called out, 'Come in.'

'Will you sign this pass, please, for Sergeant Hunter?' a nurse said, coming up to the desk.

She put a yellow slip on the desk, and the doctor said 'Oh, yes' and signed it impatiently, and she picked it up and put a little sheaf of handwritten pages in its place, and he, starting to read through these new papers with the impatience gone from his manner, said 'Ah, the ward reports' in a different voice that sounded interested and eager.

The nurse stood looking over his shoulder at the writing, most of which was her own.

'Excellent. Excellent,' Dr Pope said after a while. He glanced up at the waiting nurse and smiled at her. She was his best nurse; he had trained her himself in his own methods, and the result was entirely satisfactory. She was an invaluable and trustworthy assistant who understood what he was trying to do, approved of his technique and cooperated intelligently. 'Really excellent work,' he repeated, smiling.

She smiled back, and for a moment the identical look of gratification on the two faces gave them a curious resemblance to one another, almost as if they were near relatives, although they were not really alike at all.

'Yes,' she said, 'we're certainly getting results now. The general morale in the wards has improved enormously.' Then her face became serious again, and she said, 'If only we could get Ward Six into line'.

The smile simultaneously disappeared from the doctor's face, and a look that was more characteristic appeared there, a look of impatience and irritation. He turned the pages in front of him and reread one of them, and the irritated expression became fixed.

'Yes, I see. Ward Six again. I suppose it's that fellow Williams making a nuisance of himself as usual?'

'It's impossible to do anything with him.' The nurse's cool voice contained annoyance behind its coolness. 'He's a bad type, I'm afraid. Obstructive and stubborn. Unfortunately some of the youngsters and the less stable men are apt to be influenced by his talk. He's always stirring up discontent in the ward.'

'These confounded trouble-makers are a menace to our whole work,' Dr Pope said. 'Rebellious undesirables. I think friend Williams will have to be got rid of.' He pulled a scribbling pad across the desk and wrote the name Williams on it, pressing more heavily on the pen than he usually did so that the strokes of the letters came very black. He underlined the name with deliberation and drew a circle around it and pushed the pad back to its place and asked in a brisker tone, 'Anyone else in Six giving trouble?'

'I've been rather worried about Kling the last day or two.'

'Kling? What's he been up to?'

'He seems very depressed, Doctor.'

'You think his condition's deteriorating?'

'Well, he seems to be getting more depersonalized and generally inaccessible. There's no knowing what's in his head. It's not the language difficulty either; his English is perfectly good. But he's hardly spoken a word since that day he was put in the gardening squad and got so upset.'

'Oh, yes, the gardening incident. Odd, getting such a violent reaction there. It should give one a lead if there were time to go into it. But there isn't, of course. That's the worst of dealing with large numbers of patients as we are.' A shade of regret on the doctor's face faded out as he said to the nurse still standing beside him, 'You see far more of Kling than I do. What's your own opinion of him?'

'I think, personally, that he's got something on his mind. Something he won't talk about.'

'Make him talk, then. That's your job.'

'I've tried, of course, but it's no good. Perhaps he's afraid to talk. He's shut himself up like an oyster.'

'Oysters can be opened,' the doctor said. He twisted his chair around and smiled directly up at the good nurse he had trained. He was very pleased with her and with himself. In spite of troublesome individuals like Williams and Kling the work of the hospital was going extremely well. 'Provided, naturally, that one has the right implement with which to open them.'

He got up and stood with his back to the window, which, to be in keeping with the room's decoration, should have had satin curtains but instead was framed in dusty blackout material. He had his hands in his trouser pockets, and he was still smiling as he went on, 'We might try a little forcible opening on oyster Kling'.

The nurse nodded and made a sound of agreement and prepared to go, holding the signed pass in her hand.

'Lovely day, isn't it?' she remarked on her way, in order not to end the interview too abruptly.

Dr Pope glanced into the sunshine and turned his back on it again.

'I'll be glad when the summer's over,' he said. 'Everyone's efficiency level drops in this sort of weather. Give me the cold days when we're all really keen and on our toes.'

The nurse went out and shut the door quietly.

The doctor swung around again in his energetic fashion and opened the window as wide as it would go, looking out over grassy grounds dark with evergreens. On a hard tennis court to the right a circle of patients in shorts clumsily and apathetically threw a football about, and he watched them just long enough to observe the bored slackness of their instructor's stance and to note automatically that the man was due for a reprimand. Then he went back to his desk under the smiling doves.

As if he were somehow aware of the doctor's censorious eye, the instructor outside just then straightened up and shouted with perfunctory disgust, 'You there, Kling, or whatever your name is; wake up, for Christ's sake, can't you?'

The man who had not been ready when the ball was thrown to him, who had, in fact, altogether forgotten why he was supposed to be standing there on the hot reddish plane marked with arbitrary white lines, looked first at the instructor before bending down to the ball which had bounced off his leg and was slowly spinning on the gritty surface in front of him. He picked up the big ball and held it in both hands as though he did not know what to do with it, as though he could conceive of no possible connection between himself and this hard spherical object. Then, after a moment, he tossed it towards the man standing next to him in the ring not more than two yards away, and at once forgot it again and nothing remained of the incident in his mind except the uneasy resentment that always came now when anyone called out to him.

For many months he had been called Kling, that being the first syllable and not the whole of his name, which was too difficult for these tongues trained in a different pronunciation. To start with he had not minded the abbreviation, had even felt pleased because, like a nickname, it seemed to admit him to comradeship with the others. But now, for a long time, he had resented it. They've taken everything from me, even my name, he thought sometimes when the sullen misery settled on him. By 'they' he did not mean the men of another race with whom he shared sleeping room and food and daily routine, or any particular individuals, but just the impersonal machine that had caught and mauled him and dragged him away from the two small lakes and the mountains where his home was, far off to this flat country across the sea.

And then there was that other reason why the sound of the short syllable was disturbing.

The game, if it could be called that, came to an end, and the patients slowly dispersed. There was a little free time left before tea. Some of the men walked back to the hospital, others lighted cigarettes and stood talking in groups, several lay full length on the grass or dawdled where evergreens spread heavy mats of shade.

Kling sat down by himself on the top of a little bank. He was young, very big and broad, very well built if you didn't mind that depth of chest, dark, his hair wiry like a black dog's, arms muscled for labour, his eyes only slightly decentred. He did not look ill at all, he looked enormously strong, only his movements were all rather stiff and slow, there was a marked unnatural rigidity about the upper part of his torso because of the lately healed wound and because of that heavy thing he carried inside him.

The bank was in full sunshine. Kling sat there sweating, dark stains spreading on his singlet under the arms, sharp grasses pricking his powerful, bare, hairy legs, his breast stony feeling, waiting for time to pass. He was not consciously waiting. His apathy was so profound that it was not far removed from unconsciousness. A breeze blew and the tall grass rippled gently, but he did not know. He did not know that the sun shone. His head was bent, and the only movements about him were his slow breaths and the slowly widening stains on the singlet. His chest was hot and wet, and gloom ached in the rocky weight the black stone weighed under his breastbone, and his big blackish eyes, dilated with gloom, stared straight ahead, only blinking when the sun dazzle hurt, and sweat stood in the deep horizontal lines on his forehead.

While he sat there, a row of patients with gardening tools – spades, rakes, hoes – on their shoulders came near. They walked in single file in charge of a man walking alongside, himself in hospital clothes but with stripes on his sleeve. Kling watched them coming. All of him that still lived, resentment, gloom, misery and all his clouded confusion, slowly tightened towards alarm. He could see the polished edges of spades shining, and he shuddered, all his consciousness gathering into fear because of the danger signals coming towards him across the grass. As he watched, his breathing quickened to heave his chest up and down, and, as the gardening squad reached the foot of the bank, he made a clumsy scramble and stood up.

Standing, he heard the clink of metal and saw a shiny surface flash in the sun. The next moment he was running, stumbling stiffly, grappling the weight inside him, running from the men with the spades.

He heard the *Kling!* of his name being shouted, and again a second clattering *kling!* and running heard the spade kling-clink on the stone, he seemed to be holding it now, grasping the handle that slipped painfully in his wet hands, levering the blade under the huge ugly stone and straining finally as another frantic *kling!* came from the spade, and the toppling, heavy, leaden bulk of the stone fell and the old, mutilated face was hidden beneath, and Kling, stopping at the door of Ward Six where he had run, choking with strangled breath, while two men passing gazed at him in surprise, felt the dead mass of stone crushing his own breast.

He went into the ward and lay down on his bed and closed his eyes against the drops of sweat which trickled into the ends of his eyes. Then for a time there was nothing but the soreness of breath struggling against the stone.

This was what he had known a long while, ever since the truck had been blown thirty feet down into the ravine, and he had seen the falling stone and felt it strike, felt it smash bone, tearing through muscle, sinew and vein to lodge itself immovably in his breast. Ever since then the stone had been there inside him, and at first it had seemed a small stone, just a dead spot, a sort of numbness under the breastbone. He had told the MO about it, and the MO had laughed, saying there was no stone or possibility of a stone, and after that he had not spoken of it again, never once. But from the start he had been very uneasy, oppressed by the stone and by the heaviness that could come from it suddenly to drive away laughter and talk. He had tried not to think of the stone, but it had grown heavier and heavier until he could not think of anything else, until it crushed out everything else, and he could only carry it by making a very great effort. That was not so bad really, because with the weight of the stone crushing him he was nothing and that was not painful or frightening – it was just a waiting, and that was nothing as well. But sometimes, perhaps at the moment of going to sleep, the dead weight lifted a little, and then there were all the uncovered faces, the stone and the digging, and the old man would come back.

And so he lay very still on the bed, waiting for the deadness to overlay him, lying there in the knowledge that if the dead weight of the stone lifted to let him breathe the old man would come.

Strange how it was always this one who came and never one of the others.

The stone weight was lifting now, and Kling, who had dozed a little while after his breath had stopped struggling, woke suddenly, frightened by the return of the bloody-faced man lying in brown leaves with hairs growing out of his nostrils and a torn shirt fluttering.

That was his father who had lain dead in the room beside the Blue Lake. No, not that man. When he thought of his home he couldn't see any faces, only the jagged line of the mountains like broken eggshell against the sky, and the two lakes, the Blue Lake and the lake shaped like a harp. That, and sometimes the inn with the acid wine of the district, greenish in thick glasses, the swarming trout in the small tank on the wall, crowded sleek fish bodies slithering past the glass. But no faces ever. The stone blocked out all the home faces.

When he thought of the war it was always the digging he thought of because, seeing him so strong and used to working with a spade, they had put him on that job from the beginning; and then there were faces, wrecked or fearful or quiet or obscene faces, far too many of them, how he had laboured and toiled till his saliva ran sour, desperate to hide the faces away from the brutal light.

How many faces had he covered with earth and stones? There surely were thousands, and always thousands more waiting, and he all the time digging demented, always the compulsive urge in him like a frenzy to hide the ruined faces away. And sometimes he remembered that officer in charge of the burying party, the one who joked and sang all the time; he must have been a bit cracked really, boozed or something, but they had dug and shovelled till their hands were raw-blistered and hardly noticed the pain because of his Hey! Hi! Ho! and the jolly loud voice that he had.

There had been no singing that afternoon in the gully where the corpses, boys and old men among them, sprawled in the withered oak leaves between the rocks. Only haste then and the bitter taste in the mouth and the aching lungs, hacking the stony ground that was hard like iron to the weak bite of the spade, and the sky grey and muggy and flat and quiet. In the end someone had shouted, and the others all started running back to the truck, and he had run, too, and just then he had seen the old man lying flat on his back with blood congealing all down one side of his shattered face and the dry leaves gummed and blackening in the blood.

Kling was looking now at this object that the stone had rolled aside to reveal. There was no stone weighting him any more as he watched the object, feeling the bed shake under him as he shook and the muscles twitching in his forearms and thighs.

Then, watching the object, while his heart pounded, he saw the hairs sprouting in his father's nostrils as he lay dead on the wooden bed that was like a wagon without wheels, he saw a movement detach itself from this man in the gully, or perhaps it was the torn shirt which flapped in the wind, only there was no wind, and he did not stop to investigate but, knowing only the obsessional urge to hide at all costs that which ought not to be exposed to the level light, hoisted his spade and shoved and battered and fought the top-heavy rock until he heard a grinding crash and knew the torn face bashed out of sight, shapeless-smashed and hidden under the stone: and was it the same stone that burst his own chest and sank its black, dead heaviness in his heart?

The weight fell again now so that there was no more pain or fright and the bed did not shake; there was only the waiting that was nothingness really, and the men in blue talking and moving about the ward.

That was all that he knew, sweat slowly drying as he lay on the bed, and the old man buried mercifully by the stone. The others took no notice of Kling nor he of them, and he heard their talk and did not know that he heard until a woman's voice cut through sharp. 'Williams, and the rest of you, why are you hanging about in the ward?' He turned his head then to the nurse who had just come in; she was speaking to him, too. 'Kling, you're to go to Dr Pope after tea. You'd better get up and make yourself decent', and he saw her pale, cold eyes linger on him as she went out of the door.

'Get up and make yourself decent,' the man called Williams said. 'That's a way to talk to a fellow who's sick.'

Kling said nothing but looked up at him, waiting.

'To hell with them,' Williams said. 'To hell with the whole set-up. Bloody racket to get sick men back into the army. Cannon fodder, that's all they care about. Taking advantage of poor mugs like us. Pep talks. Pills to pep you up. Dope to make you talk. Putting chaps to sleep and giving them electric shocks and Christ knows what. Lot of bloody guinea pigs, that's what we are. Bloody, isn't it?'

Kling was staring at him with blank eyes.

'Look at Kling here,' Williams said. 'Any fool can see he's as sick as hell. Why can't they leave him in peace? Why should he go back into their bloody army? This isn't his country anyway. Why should he fight for it?'

From the far reaches of his non-being Kling looked at the faces around him. They were all looking at him, but they had no meaning. Williams had no meaning any more than the others. But he heard Williams go on.

'Damned Gestapo methods. Spying and snooping round listening to talk. Bitches of nurses. Why the hell do we stand for it?'

A bell was ringing, and the patients started to move out of the ward. Kling, staring up, saw the shapes of their meaningless faces receding from him. He looked at Williams, who was still there, and Williams looked back at him, smiling, and said, 'Coming to tea, chum?' And in the words Kling half recognized something forgotten and long-lost, and some corresponding thing in him which had died long ago almost revived itself; but the stone was too heavy for that resurrection, and he could not know that what he wanted to do was to smile.

'So long, then, if you're stopping here,' Williams said. He pulled a packet of Weights out of his pocket and put a cigarette on the bed beside Kling's hand which did not move. 'Don't let that bastard of a doctor put anything over on you,' Kling heard Williams, walking towards the door, call back to him as he went.

Kling did not smoke the cigarette or pick it up even; but after a time rose, and with those stiff motions which seemed to be rehearsing some exercise not well remembered, washed, dressed himself in shirt and blue trousers, combed his thick hair and went along corridors to the door upon which was fastened the doctor's name.

There was a bench outside the door, and he sat down on it, waiting. The passage was dark because the windows had been coated with black paint for the blackout. Nothing moved in the long, dark, silent passage at the end of which Kling sat alone on the bench. He sat there bending forward, his hands clasped between his knees, his red tie dangling, his eyes fixed on the ground. He did not wonder what would happen behind the door. He waited, without speculation or awareness of waiting. It was all the same to him, outside or here or in the ward; he did not notice, it made no difference to his waiting.

A nurse opened the door and called him, and he got up and stepped forward, and looking past her along the wall of the corridor thought, How many stones there are in this place; so many faces and stones, and lost the thought before it meant anything and went into the room.

'I want you to lie on the couch,' Dr Pope told him. 'We're going to give you a shot of something that will make you feel a bit sleepy. Quite a pleasant feeling. It won't hurt at all.'

Obedient, null, with that unnatural stiffness, Kling laid himself down.

Lying on the high couch he looked at the exuberant ceiling without surprise. The flowers and the crowding cherubic faces did not seem any more strange to him than anything else. The ceiling did not concern him any more than the doctor concerned him. Nothing concerned him except the heaviness in his breast. He waited, looking at the doctor as if he had never seen him before, the nurse busy with swab and spirit and tourniquet, and he felt far off on his arm the tourniquet tightening, the bursting pressure of flesh against tightening fabric and then the small sharp sting as the needle entered the vein.

'Just try to relax,' the doctor said, watching, while the fluid in the hypodermic went down, the blank waiting face with wide-open extremely dilated eyes.

He smiled his professional smile of encouragement and looked from the face to the chest and the massive shoulders bulked rigid under the white shirt that they stretched tight, at the clenched strong hands, the rough blue cloth strained on the tensed thighs, the stiffly upthrust boots not neatly laced, and back to the blank face again. He noticed on the face how the deep tan of the outdoor years was starting to turn yellowish as it slowly faded inside hospital walls.

'Well, how do you feel now?' he asked, smiling, the man who stared up at him without answering.

'I want you to talk, Kling,' he said. 'I want you to tell me what's worrying you.'

Kling, his patient, looked away from him and up at the ceiling.

'What is it you've got on your mind?' asked the doctor.

Kling stared upwards without speaking, and now his limbs started twitching a little.

'You'll feel better after you've talked,' Dr Pope said.

The nurse finished the long injection and withdrew the syringe adroitly. A single drop of blood oozed from the pierced vein and she dabbed a shred of cotton wool on to it and silently carried her paraphernalia into the background and stood watching.

'You've got to tell me what's making you miserable,' the doctor said, speaking loud. He bent down and put his hand on Kling's shoulder and said loudly and very distinctly, close to his ear, 'You are very miserable, aren't you?'

Kling looked at him with his wide, black, lost animal's eyes and felt the hand on his shoulder. His shoulder twitched, and something inside him seemed to be loosening, he felt sick in his stomach, and a sleepy strangeness was coming up at him out of nowhere, turning him tired or sick.

'Why are you miserable?' he heard the question. 'Something happened to you, didn't it? Something you can't forget. What was that thing?'

Kling saw the doctor standing far too close, bending down almost on top of him. The hand that had hold of his shoulder gripped hard like a trap, the distorted face looked monstrous, foreshortened and suspended beneath painted faces, the eyes glaring, the threat of the mouth opening and shutting. Kling groaned, turning his head from one side to the other to escape from the eyes, but the eyes would not let him go. He felt the strangeness of sleep or sickness or death moving up on him, and then something gave way in his chest, the stone shifted and sleep came forward to the foot of the couch, and he groaned again, louder, clutching his chest, crumpling the shirt and the red tie over his breastbone.

'Was it something bad that was done to you?' he heard the doctor's voice shout in his ear.

He felt himself turning and twisting on the hard bed, twisting away from the eyes and the voice and the gripping hand that was shaking him now. He shut his eyes to escape, but a salt prick of tears or sweat forced them open, he did not know where he was or what was happening to him, and he was afraid. He was very frightened with the strange sleep so near him, he wanted to call for help, it was hard for him to keep silent. But somewhere in the midst of fear existed the thought, They've taken everything; let them not take my silence. And the queer thing was that Williams was somehow a part of this, his smile, the cigarette and what he had spoken.

'Was it something bad that *you* did?' Kling heard.

He did not feel the hand that was shaking his shoulder. He only felt his face wet, and on the other side of sleep a voice kept on moaning while another voice shouted. But he could not listen because, just then, the stone moved quite away from his breast and sleep came up and laid its languid head on his breast in place of the stone.

He tried to look at the strange sleep, to know it, but it had no form, it simply rested sluggishly on him like gas, and all he could see above was a cloud of faces; the entire earth was no graveyard great enough for so many, nor was there room to remember a smile or a cigarette or a voice any more.

The old man was there and had been for some time, not sprawled in leaves now but standing, bent forward, listening; and Kling knew that this time something must pass between them, there was something which must be said by him, in extenuation, or in entreaty, to which the old man must reply, although what it was that had to be said, or what words would be found to express it, did not appear yet.

The old man bent over him and blood dripped on to his face and he could not move because of what lay on his breast, and when the old man saw he could not move he bent lower still, and Kling could see the tufts of bristly hairs in his father's nostrils. He knew he would have to speak soon, and, staring wildly, with the old man's face almost on his, he could see the side of the face that was only a bloodied hole, and he heard a sudden frantic gasp and gush of words in his own language, and that was all he heard because at that moment sleep reached up and covered over his face.

Dr Pope and the nurse had both seen that Kling was going to start talking. The doctor had seen it coming for about half a minute and waited intently. The nurse looked expectant. When the first sounds came both of them had moved forward at once, and the doctor had bent lower over his patient, but now they stepped back from the couch.

'I was afraid that might happen,' Dr Pope said in his impatient voice. 'Damned annoying. I suppose there's no one in the place who could translate?'

'I'm afraid not,' the nurse said.

'Exasperating,' the doctor said. 'So we shan't get anything out of him after all.'

'I'm afraid not,' the nurse said again.

'Most frustrating and disappointing,' said Dr Pope. 'Oh well, it's no good trying to work on him now.'

THE GANNETS

IT WAS SPRINGTIME, A windy day. I had walked a long way on the cliffs by a path that I did not know. Gannets were diving like snow falling into the sea, pursuing a shoal of fish that kept parallel with the shore. I'm not certain now whether I walked so far in order to watch the gannets or to explore the coast or simply because it was a bright afternoon.

After winding for a long time between low bushes and rocks, the path suddenly began to climb steeply over a headland. Seeing the difficult track ahead made me realize that I was tired and that I had already come much further than I had intended. From the position of the sun I knew that it must be getting late. The sensible thing would have been to turn back then, especially as the gannets, which I had perhaps been following unconsciously, were vanishing around the rocky point shaped like the snout of a huge saurian. But instead of starting the long walk home I kept on, telling myself that I might as well see what lay beyond the head since I had come so far. It was quite a stiff climb; the path was slippery with pine needles and loose stones, and I was breathless by the time I got to the top. There was nothing about the view from the crest, either, to justify the effort of getting there. However far I looked I could see only a vista of the same yellowish rocky cliffs topped with pine trees and scrub which had been in front of my eyes the whole afternoon.

A few yards away, in a hollow of the downward slope, was a dilapidated wooden shack. At first I thought it must be some old boatshed or deserted fisherman's hut. The half-ruined place, apparently only held together by roughly nailed boards and wire and patched with beaten-out tins, seemed much too ramshackle to be inhabited. But then I saw signs of occupancy: a heap of fresh potato peelings thrown outside the door, a few indescribably sordid rags hanging from the crazy posts of what had once been a fence.

I stood there in the wind for a minute, resting and getting my breath after the climb. And as I was wondering how any human being could be so unfortunate or so degraded as to live in such squalor, five or six children appeared and clustered together staring out to sea. They were, like the hovel, indescribably squalid, almost naked, hideous with neglect. They pointed towards the sea where the gannets on this side of the point were diving much closer in, with folded wings hurtling like bolts through the air, to strike the water one after the other in jets of spray. I could not hear much of what the children were saying, but it seemed from certain words and from their gestures that they expected the birds to come near. I waited to see what would happen. We all gazed at the gannets, which were now no longer diving or searching the waves but planing portentously towards us with infrequent wing strokes. And sure enough I was presently half deafened by a storm of harsh cries immediately overhead. Long black-tipped wings hid the sun, shadowing everything; only the cold round eyes and the fierce beaks glittered. And hardly had the flock sighted the children than they seemed to be menacing them, screaming headlong towards them in horrid haste. I shouted some sort of warning, urging the children to run into the house. They took no notice. I saw their looks full of excitement and anticipation but without any amazement. They seemed to be taking part in a procedure well known to them. Already the gannets were swooping upon one of them, the smallest of the group, whom two of the others dragged along by her stick-like arms. And it was beyond all possibility of doubt that this miserable little creature was the victim among them, already dedicated to the birds. Not terror alone gave such a shocking blankness to her lifted face, darkened by two great holes, bloodied pits from which the eyes had already been torn. I shouted again and began running with an idea of beating the gannets off with my hands, but then I must have stumbled and fallen heavily. I must have been stunned by the fall on the jagged rock, for when I got up the cliff was silent and lonely, the wind had died down and the sun was sinking behind sullen bars of cloud edged with fire.

How did all this atrocious cruelty ever get into the world, that's what I often wonder. No one created it, no one invoked it, and no saint, no genius, no dictator, no millionaire, no, not God's son himself, is able to drive it out.

OUR CITY

'I did believe, and do still, that the end of our city will be with Fire and Brimstone from above.'

I

HOW OFTEN ONE HEARS our city spoken of as 'cruel'. In fact, this adjective is used so frequently that in many people's minds cruelty has become accepted as the city's most typical and outstanding attribute, whereas there are in existence a great variety of other qualities, probably equally characteristic and certainly just as remarkable.

To my mind, one of the most astonishing things about the city is its plurality. In my own personal experience, for example, it has, during a comparatively short space of time, displayed three distinct manifestations of its complex being. And if it is possible for one individual in one brief period to witness three such changes, just imagine the astronomical number of different forms in which our city is bound to appear through the centuries to the millions of its inhabitants.

In my case, the first metamorphosis was, I think, the most unexpected; for who, even among the unprejudiced, would expect the city to show itself as an octopus? Yet that is exactly what happened. Slowly, with deliberation, and at the same time as it seemed almost languidly, a blackish tentacle was unfurled which travelled undeviatingly across the globe to the remote antipodean island where I imagined myself secure. I shall not forget the tentacle's deceptive semi-transparency, something like that dark Swedish glass which contains tints both purple and black while still keeping translucence. The tentacle had the same insubstantial, ethereal look, but it had also a strength many times greater than that of the strongest steel.

The second metamorphosis was, by comparison with the first, almost predictable. It was, in a sense, logical, and, although I won't go so far as to say that I actually anticipated it, I certainly recognized its inevitability when it appeared. As a matter of fact, I believe I really did, if not consciously or completely, at least in some obscure, inchoate way, foresee it; although it's difficult to be quite sure of this after the event. We all of us know from films or pictures or the posters of the Society for the Prevention of Cruelty to Animals, those hideous toothed traps, sadistic jaws which snap upon the delicate leg or paw of some soft-furred wild creature, mangling the flesh and splintering the fragile bones and clamping the victim to a slow, agonizing death. There is even a sort of resemblance between the serrated blade as it must appear shearing down on its prey and the ferocious skyline of a city partially laid waste.

With regard to the third metamorphosis, I am in an uncertain position. To me this aspect of the city's character, although less clearly in sequence than the second, still is quite comprehensible and far from surprising in view of what had gone before. But to an outsider, someone from another part of the world, I can see that it may well seem the most astonishing manifestation of all. 'How can a city be a judge at one and the same time?' I can imagine such a man asking. 'A judge, what's more, who not only arraigns the criminal, sets up the court, conducts the trial and passes sentence but actually sees that the sentence is carried out.'

To such a person I can only reply that I have no explanation to give him. These things are not well understood, and doubtless there's some good reason why we don't understand them. The most satisfactory attitude is to accept the facts as they are without too much probing, perhaps simultaneously working out some private thesis of one's own to account for them.

No, I can't explain how our city can be at one time a judge, at another a trap, at another an octopus. Nor have I any way of elucidating the sentence passed on me, which is really two sentences, mutually exclusive but running concurrently: the sentence of banishment from the city and of imprisonment in it. You may wonder how I have the heart to keep on at all in such a hopeless position. Indeed, there often are times when I'm practically in despair, when the contradiction seems too bitter and senseless and incomprehensible to be borne. All that keeps me going then, I think, is the hope that some time or other I may by chance come upon the solution, that one half of the contradiction will somehow dissolve into the other, or the sentence as a whole be modified or even remitted. It's no good approaching these obscure matters systematically. All one can do is to go on living, if possible, and moving a little, tentatively, as occasion offers, first in one direction and then in another. Like that a solution may ultimately be found, as in the case of those puzzles made of wires intertwined, which suddenly and by a purely accidental manipulation fall apart into two halves.

II

There's a street near where I live which is very ugly. It's not a slum street but part of what is called a respectable cheap neighbourhood. The people who live there are quite poor. The refugee woman who works in the library rents a room in this street. She has taken refuge there. I should have thought myself that it was more a place to escape from.

It's not only the small yellowish-grey houses which are ugly: the actual roadway that pitches not steeply uphill, the lamp-posts, the squat air-raid shelter, even the gutters, all seem to have an air of meanness and malevolence which is frightening. The street has a smell, too. It is, as far as I can describe it, a sour smell, with spite in it.

A smell of asphalt, of dustbins not emptied often enough and spite. The people who walk in the street look spiteful, too; they glance at you resentfully as they pass, as if they would like to do you an injury. They look at you as if they wished you were at their mercy. I should hate to be handed over to the mercy of the people in this street. Even the children who dart up and down have faces like spiteful gnomes. A little girl in a plaid dress pushes past me; her limp, uncombed hair brushes my arm, and that moment, from just underneath my elbow, she lets out a shrill screech that pierces the whole afternoon. I feel as if a hobgoblin had jabbed a long pin through my ear.

The bald, excrescent shelter which I'm now passing has a curious morbid look, like some kind of tumour that has stopped being painful and hardened into a static, permanent lump. It reminds me of one of those chronic swellings you sometimes see on a person's neck which has been there so long that no one but a stranger notices it any more. The entrance to the shelter is screened with wire netting. I look through. The inside of the place is unclean.

Now, something quite extraordinary occurs in the street. A small dog comes around the corner, running after his mistress. Yes, actually a dog; what a relief. And, what's more, it's a dog of that particular aristocratic, antique breed, half lion, half marmoset, from which, rather than from any other species, I would choose a companion if ever again it became possible for me to know such happiness as companionship with a dog.

This little dog, coloured like a red squirrel, runs with the gay abandonment peculiar to his race, his plumy tail streaming behind and seeming to beat the pavement to the rhythm of his elastic and bounding movements. How can I explain my emotion at the sight of that small, heraldic-looking beast careering so buoyantly? The appearance of these dogs when they run has always seemed to me quite amazingly intrepid and lively, at the same time both brave and amusing – even faintly absurd – yet somehow exceedingly dashing and debonair, almost heroic, in the style of diminutive Quixotes launching themselves without the least hesitation upon the enormously dangerous world.

The lion-dog runs forward with all his racial gallantry and *élan* into that ugly street smelling of asphalt, sourness and spite. It comes to this, then, as I see it. One must try to live up to the dog's standard. That's what one must aim at.

III

How blue the sky is this morning, as if summer had kindly approved the date set for putting the clocks on another hour. It's only the fourth of April, and now we've already got double summertime. Today might easily have been foggy like it was most of last week; it might have been pouring with rain or blowing a gale; there might even have been a snowstorm. But, thank goodness, the weather is perfect. There isn't so much to be thankful for these days; the people walking uphill to the candle-spired church must often be hard put to it to find suitable subjects for thanksgiving in their prayers. Today, though, everybody can thank God for the fine weather. And people with gardens, how happy they must be: they've got an extra cause to give thanks with the daffodils springing bright everywhere and the blossom coming out on the fruit trees just as prettily as it does in countries which are at peace. Overnight, as it seems, the chestnut buds have burst into harmless miniature flares, beautifully green. All the trees which have been dull and dormant so long are now suddenly lit up by these miraculous green fires, gentle beacons of hope, quietly and graciously burning. Oh, how blue the sky is. The barrage balloons look foolish and rather gay, like flocks of silver-paper kites riding high up there in the blue.

In the garden of the small house below the church an old cherry tree is just on the point of blooming. Thousands of tiny white buds, still close and firm, tremble all over the branches among golden-green leaves the size of a mouse's ear. On some of the upper boughs, more exposed to the sun, the blossom is out already, and here the open petals cluster so thickly that it looks as if snow showers had caught and lingered among the young leaves. A few early bees have found out the cherry tree and are working busily over the white flowers.

The foreign girl who lives in the little house leans out of the window. She's quite close to the cherry blossom, she could almost touch the starry sprays if she leaned out a little further. A brightness comes on her face, reflected perhaps from the bloom. Or perhaps the humming bees and the twittering of the birds remind her of home. Perhaps she suddenly remembers hearing those cheerful sounds under a stronger sun.

The girl is in no hurry to leave the window. For quite a long time she leans out with her arms on the sill, and the wind lightly stirs the fair hair beside her face which in spite of its bright look somehow gives an impression of sadness. From where she stands she can see over the garden wall into the street of grey quiet houses leading uphill to the church. It is the hour of the morning when in ordinary times the church bells would be ringing. There are no bells now, and the few people on their way to the service walk slowly, separated from one another, in dark clothes that look too heavy for the spring day. At the open door of the house opposite a woman and a little boy are watching the people disappear one by one into the church. When the last one is out of sight the mother puts her hand on the child's head, turns him gently back into the house with her and closes the door behind them without a sound.

The street is quite empty now under the blue sky across which a cloud in the shape of a swan is airily floating.

In a moment a girl comes around the corner, walking fast. She is dark eyed, very slender, and well dressed; her high heels tap merrily as she hurries along. She sees her friend at the window, waves to her and calls out a greeting. The foreign girl runs down to meet her, and soon they are sitting on the grass where a sprinkle of white petals has yet to fall. How happy they seem together under the cherry tree, talking and smiling often; the dark eyes gleam in the sun, the grey eyes reflect the tender blue of the sky. The dark girl gives news of her husband, a soldier fighting far off in the desert, from whom she has just had a letter. While she speaks of him her face is lively and beautiful. The foreigner leans forward with eagerness, rejoicing in her friend's pleasure.

Something catches her attention so that she turns her head. Look, a butterfly, she calls out. The first butterfly of the year. The first one I've seen since I left my home.

And then, as she watches the wavering flight of the pretty red-brown butterfly, the animation dies out of her face, her eyes lose their blueness and slowly darken with tears. The other girl, too, becomes grave; the words she is saying falter, dead before they are spoken; the fragile happiness which these two had nourished between them vanishes like the butterfly whose uncertain, frail wings seem to be at the mercy of the first breath of wind.

It is not only the exile whose cheeks have become wet, and although they are both conscious of this they say nothing about it, they don't speak of anything sad but quickly start talking about some clouds which are coming up shaped not like swans but like small shying horses. Soon both the girls are smiling often again. Probably it's only an illusion that their voices no longer sound quite so gay. Out of doors, in the lovely spring weather, how could anyone help feeling gay? So beautifully blue the sky is; the cherry blossom so white.

IV

The clock by my bed has a dial that shines in the dark. It is a small white clock with a shutter that slides over its face when it starts out on a journey. This clock has accompanied me on many tremendous journeys. It has been stowed carefully away and muffled against damage in the gales of northern oceans; the spray of tropical seas has tarnished its metal parts; from beside many beds it has patiently watched with me the solemn march of the constellations of two hemispheres.

Now it stands with the same patience at this improbable city bedside. It ticks in the same unflurried, impersonal fashion. Its tick does not sound either friendly or unfriendly: it has a sound which suggests impartiality. It is an impartial, scientific observer, this clock, quietly recording into eternity all that passes in front of its face. In spite of our long association, the clock and I are not on intimate terms; my feeling for the clock is one of respect more than cordiality.

Just now the hands of the clock stand at half past two. They gleam greenishly in the dark. I've been asleep for an hour. A minute or so ticks away. Then there is noise. The sirens wail up and down my room with howling violence. It always happens like that, it's always the same; it's not the sirens that wake me, I always wake up a minute or two before the alert actually sounds. The siren noise comes to an end; other noises begin. Mobile guns grind elephantinely over me. A plane buzzes around my head. Outside the black windows the searchlights climb questing. I can feel the broad beams sawing and the narrow beams scissoring through my nerves. Then suddenly, from far away over the city, dull, muffled, heavy noise. Pandemonium is starting up; is coming nearer and nearer, implacably; is here, ultimately, on top of me. The darkness explodes into thunderous tumult. Through it all I catch the slither of some small object falling inside my room. I put out my hand to the switch, and, incredible as it seems, the light goes on just as usual. In the calm yellow light I see that it is, of course, the picture on the chest-of-drawers that has slipped on the polished wood and fallen down on its face. It always happens like that, every time it's the same; the vibration always makes the picture fall down. The noise batters the night with unappeasable fury. The whole night outside is rent and rocking in all directions. I cover my ears in a vain attempt to shut out some of the din; in particular, there's one excruciating sound which resembles, magnified to the nth degree, the screech of tearing canvas that I desperately try to exclude.

The noise makes me feel inexpressibly lonely. I am quite alone in the little house, alone with the clock whose tick I can no longer distinguish. I have the impression that I'm the only living soul in the midst of this fiendish hullaballoo. Can there really be other human beings out there in the city? Impossible to imagine that people are connected in any way with the racket that's going on. It's an absolutely inhuman excess of noise, the rage of the city itself. Our city itself is ravening at the night.

Like a lighted bubble my room floats irresponsibly in the shattering noise. The curtains flutter a little, but the pale-blue carpet doesn't turn a hair. It's a fact; the pale-blue carpet actually still covers the floor from wall to wall. The din seems incessant, but there must be infinitesimal pauses, for at some moment I am aware of the clock ticking attentively. I hear the bottles on the dressing-table snigger against one another. Ages go past like this.

At last things grow quieter: the noise is diminishing, retreating, petering out. Planes snarl frantically overhead, then zoom off, away from the city. Someone walks quickly along the street outside with heavy steps: a warden, perhaps. So there are people alive, moving about in the city. The clock goes on ticking, a diligent and indefatigable recorder. Presently the all-clear sounds, interminably, like a boy seeing how long he can hold his breath. At last even that noise stops, and there is immeasurable relief. Very carefully, being as quiet as possible, I switch out the light.

The noise is over. But now something begins to happen that is in its way as sensational, as appalling. Through the darkness of the blacked-out windows I am aware of an indescribable movement throughout the city, a soundless spinning of motion in the streets and among the ruins, an unseen upward surge of building: the silence industriously, insecurely, building itself up. The silence gathers itself together in the parks and the squares and the gaps and the empty houses. Like a spider's web rapidly woven, the frail edifice mounts up quickly towards the moon. Soon the precarious work is finished, the whole city is roofed, covered in with silence, as if lying under a black cloche. The tension is frightful. With compressed lips and foreheads lined with anxiety every citizen crouches uneasily, peering up at the transparent black bell of silence hanging over our city. Is it going to break?

V

What a heartbreaking contrariness there is in this world. It seems as if things were deliberately, cunningly planned to cause one the maximum amount of chagrin. Take this little house where I live now, for instance. What could be more inappropriate to a person in my predicament than these two pleasant rooms, one of which is actually carpeted in pale velvety blue? There's something shocking and painful in the mere thought of associating myself in my present unhappy state with anything so frivolous as a blue carpet. And yet there have been periods of my life when a place like this would have suited me perfectly. Then, of course, I was unable to find anything of the sort and was forced to exist in some gloomy setting as out of keeping with my circumstances at the time as this cottage is with my present position.

I sometimes wonder what induces the authorities to allow me to stay here, in comfort, with pictures, with lamps. Probably it won't be permitted much longer. There have been indications lately that a change is contemplated. Who knows from what stony barrack, what freezing cell, I may before long find myself looking back on all this with nostalgic regret? Quite likely it's with that very object that I'm left here at present – just so that the change, when it comes, shall be all the more intolerable. Oh yes, they're ingenious enough for anything, those into whose hands we are committed.

Certainly it was a subtle finesse to decree that the first bitter months of my sentence should be served in an environment which continually seems to be making a mockery of my sufferings with its incongruous gaiety. Often there are days now when I feel absolutely desperate, when the weight of my burden seems far too heavy to bear. And on these days the place takes a callous delight in flaunting itself, as if determined to draw my attention to the fact that not I but some happy, privileged being, perhaps a charming young actress with many lovers, really ought to be living here. The very pictures on the walls, portraying as they do light-hearted columbines and nymphs in amorous poses, smile down on me with cynical mockery.

The fact that the windows look out upon trees and gardens is part of the cruel design. For in this way I am sometimes tricked into forgetting the city; I fall into the trap of believing that I am free, that there is open country outside and not streets and ruins. And then comes the terrible moment when it occurs to me that the city is still there, and I pace from corner to corner, of course finding nothing but still blindly searching for something that might not reject me, in the dreadful destitution of the condemned. How everything in the rooms jeers at me then. The walls shake with laughter. The painted houris sneer, curling their rosy lips at the idea that I should still be looking for mercy after all my misdeeds. Not even the sparrows that I've just fed with crumbs from the window restrain their ridicule but fly away tittering. And the carpet, the blue carpet: the pale-blue carpet finds it necessary to spread out its softness under my feet in sheerest derision.

VI

It's queer that I can't get out of the way of walking about. Here in the city, where few people except eccentrics ever walk unless forced to do so, I still don't seem to be able to break this countrified habit. A part of the distance between the cottage in which I sleep and the place where I work is occupied by an area without houses, a stretch of heath or rough parkland, where children play and dogs run about sniffing the grass. Every afternoon, for some time now, I've walked across this stretch of land which is partly wooded and partly covered with thickets of gorse and bramble. There's a pleasant path here that runs through the trees. At a particular turn of the path a silver birch bends over it, as if shaking out a threadbare green curtain.

Today it was cooler and darker than usual under the trees. I stopped in an open clearing and looked up at the sky. The segment that lay behind me, towards the west, was full of a limpid light; the part ahead darkened softly with blowing clouds. Chromium against gunmetal, the barrage balloons on which the light fell embossed themselves on the tarnished shield of the sky. And above them, much higher up, so high as to seem no larger than a migration of birds, a huge formation of bombers was steadily travelling towards its distant night-time objective. Sometimes blurred, sometimes flashing with brightness, the machines in outlandish beauty pursued their lonely and awful course, filling the whole atmosphere with a muted thunder.

Why was it so dark and chilly down in the wood? I thought at first that I must be later than usual. And then it suddenly dawned on me that this hour which up to now had been afternoon had today slipped over the boundary into evening, and that the brown, scorched look of the trees came, not from drought, but from approaching winter. In the thinning foliage, here and there certain yellow leaves trembled and said 'Death' with a frightened voice.

A nondescript, paunchy man sauntered through the wood, whistling to a black dog. Then two very ordinary middle-aged people came around the curve under the silver birch. The man wore an officer's uniform but was not at all martial-looking: he held his cap under the arm farther from his companion, and from the hand at the end of this arm there dangled a string bag containing packages and a bottle of milk. His hair was grey and quite thin; his tunic did not fit very well, and he seemed to sag a little at the knees as he walked. The woman with him looked like a housekeeper in a shapeless fawn coat and a serviceable brown hat that had never been gay. Quite suddenly and spontaneously these two people turned to one another and linked hands and walked on swinging their joined hands lightly and proudly between them like young lovers. They could not repress the timid joy in their faces and smiled at everything that they passed, at me, at the dog, at the trees. I began to make an effort to master myself as soon as I saw them, otherwise I must have burst into tears or thrown myself on the ground or started tearing my clothes with abandoned fingers. When one sees people like this so happy it is hard indeed to endure one's sentence. Why, even a paunchy, nondescript man has his black dog which accompanies him unquestioningly in faithful devotion wherever he chooses to go.

VII

Our city is full of the troops of a foreign army. When I first arrived here from the other side of the world I couldn't tell whether these soldiers were friends or invaders, and even now I'm equally at a loss.

Wherever money is being spent these men in their costly and elegant uniforms are to be found, in theatres, bars, restaurants, stores, buying the best of everything and conducting themselves in a lavish way far beyond the resources of the citizens who are pushed quite into the background. Very often it's impossible to get what one wants – whether it's a meal or a drink or a seat at an entertainment or some article in a shop – because these people have bought up everything. And as for taxis and cars – well, the drivers seem to have placed their vehicles exclusively at the disposal of the foreign soldiers and their bottomless purses.

Are they, in fact, allies or enemies? Often enough one hears bitter remarks which suggest the latter alternative. But if that were the case wouldn't the hostility of the citizens take some more dynamic form than mere acrimonious grumbling? And then, it must be admitted, the conduct of the strangers isn't what one traditionally expects of a conquering army. Beyond the fact of their ubiquitousness and the way in which they monopolize all amenities, they appear not to interfere with our city at all. They have not, for example, taken over control of any of the public services or made any attempt to alter the laws or impose their own restrictions.

Occasionally, although this doesn't often happen, one sees them going about with the local people, usually girls they've picked up somewhere or perhaps a youngster impressed by their spending powers. Or one catches sight of a group of their high-ranking officers formally escorted by a party of our dignitaries through the doors of a solemn official building.

One's natural impulse, of course, is to question somebody and settle things once and for all. But a person in my situation can't be too careful; I have to think twice about whatever I do, even about such a simple thing as asking a question. The last thing I want is to draw attention to myself in any way. And then, with our complex system of regulations, continually changing from day to day, how is one to know what is permitted? If I were to make a mistake the result might be fatal for me. A single false step might easily end in disaster. Besides, even if I were so reckless as to stop a passer-by and make my inquiry, how can I be sure that he'd give me an answer? As likely as not he would merely look at me suspiciously and pass on, even if he did not actually lodge a complaint against me. For a passionate secretiveness characterizes the inhabitants of our city. It simply isn't worth while taking such a chance. I'd rather remain uncertain.

It's not as if the foreigners were constantly being brought to my notice, either; in the way I live now, I often pass two or three days without seeing a single one of them.

In the beginning it was quite different. Before I was directed to the work which now occupies me, while I had time on my hands to wander about the city, I naturally gave a good deal of attention to the strange soldiers whom I saw everywhere lounging about, apparently as idle as I was myself. In those days I had some peculiar notions about them. Laughable as it may seem, I developed the idea that these men were in some way linked to me, that there was something in common between us, like a distant blood relationship. I, the city's outcast and prisoner, seemed to feel with these foreigners a connection, sympathetic perhaps, which did not exist where the citizens were concerned. Often, as I glanced at the strangers, their large, tanned, dispassionate, ruminative faces would touch some recollection in me; I would suddenly be reminded of the faces of friends in a far-distant country, the conviction would sweep over me that I was here confronting members of a race that had once been most dear to me, like brothers. And this emotion was so strong that it was all I could do to restrain myself from making an appeal of some kind to them in my desolation.

I remember particularly one such occasion. I was waiting for a bus in one of the main streets when my eyes wandered idly towards a foreign captain sitting at a small table outside a restaurant. Immediately the sensation I have described came over me, but with such intense poignancy that it was as if I had suddenly caught sight of a beloved and well-known face among the indifferent crowd. Instinctively, hardly knowing what I was doing, I started moving towards this man, some incoherent phrase already forming itself in my head. Heaven knows what I might have said to him, what fantastic supplication for comfort, for aid, I might have poured out to him. But precisely at that moment, as if at a given signal, he got up in a leisurely manner and strolled away. It seemed to me that only a few yards separated us, that I had only to take one or two steps in order to catch up with him. And, crazily, I did start forward, meaning to overtake him. Perhaps he had entered one of the neighbouring shops, perhaps he had started to cross the street and was hidden by passing cars, in any case, he had already vanished completely. The pavement, as usual, was crowded with the strange uniforms, so much smarter and better-fitting than ours; and for the next few moments I kept staring distractedly into one and then another of those unknown faces, some of which looked back at me I believe not unsympathetically. But not one of them was in the least like the face for which I was searching, and which I suppose I am never to see again.

Perhaps it was lucky for me that I was denied the opportunity of speaking; but how can I be sure, having no means of obtaining information about the soldiers? So I must go on in uncertainty, even though foreign eyes still sometimes seem to gaze at me in passing with a look of fraternal compassion and understanding, encouraging me to do the thing which I most fear doing.

VIII

Like a recurrent dream, the following scene repetitiously unfolds itself: I am sitting in a bureau, putting forward my case; it is the nine-hundred-and-ninety-ninth station of my tedious Calvary. In front of me stands the usual large desk covered with papers and telephones; this one has on it, too, a small notice, neatly printed and framed like a calendar, saying, 'If danger becomes imminent during an alert the bureau will be closed.' Behind the desk sits the usual bureaucrat; this time it's a big man with curly hair and a pin-stripe suit who confronts me discouragingly.

My voice goes on and on like a gramophone record. I'm not listening to it, I don't pay any attention to the words coming out of my mouth. The whole speech became mechanical ages ago and drearily reels itself off without any assistance from me. Instead of associating myself with the dismal recitation, I stare out of the window from which it looks as if some destructive colossus had been stamping upon our city, trampling down whole blocks and boroughs with his gigantic jackboots. Acres and acres of flattened rubble spread out spacious and so simplified that the eye is baffled and it's impossible to tell which objects are near and which are remote. It's not possible to say where the cheek of the earth starts to curve or where the unsuppressed bright river loops over the bulge down to the oceans and the archipelagos on the underside of the world. The few buildings which remain intact in this vicinity stand about self-consciously amidst the harmonious demolition. They look singularly uncomfortable and as if they had taken fright at their own conspicuousness: one can see they do not quite recognize themselves in such embarrassing circumstances. They stand there at a loss, wishing to retire into the decent collective security which they dimly remember as being their proper place; or else to lose definition by amalgamating with the undetailed collapse all around them.

Just to the side of the window, a wing of the building from which I am looking juts out sharply at right angles, and here, on the roof and in the interior, I can see men repairing some damage it has sustained. From a gaping black tear in the wall a workman in shirt-sleeves is starting to lower a bucket down the façade. I notice his face contracted in concentration; he's so close that I can distinguish the hairs on his arms which are straining away at the rope as he lowers the bucket with immense care, as if there were a baby inside it. What on earth has he got in the bucket? If only I could find that out perhaps everything would suddenly come right for me. While my lips automatically go on shaping the phrases of my petition, I am leaning forward and craning my neck in the hope of having a peep inside the bucket which is now hidden from me by the window-sill.

Suddenly I'm snatched away from my preoccupation by the angry voice of the bureaucrat; my own voice snaps off into startled silence in mid-sentence, as if the needle had abruptly been lifted off the record.

'What's the good of coming here with this rigmarole, wasting my time?' the man at the desk is exclaiming. 'Surely you know we don't deal with matters of that sort in my department – what you need is a public adviser – he's the person you ought to go to.'

'An adviser?' I repeat, in amazement. I can hardly believe my ears. 'Is someone in my position allowed to consult an adviser, then?'

For some reason my astonishment makes the bureaucrat still more indignant. He thumps the desk with his fist so that the telephones give a nervous, frustrated, tinkle, the pens shake apprehensively in their tray.

'I've no patience with people like you,' he shouts rudely. 'How do you ever expect to get your affairs in order when you haven't got even enough sense to find out the proper procedure?'

He gets up and approaches me around the desk, and I hastily jump off my chair and back away from him in alarm.

'Be off with you!' he cries. His face is suffused with scarlet rage. If he were wearing an apron he would certainly flap it at me, but as it is he can only shoo me towards the door with his hands.

I retreat as fast as I can from the loud, angry voice and the red face bearing down on me threateningly. So it is that I never discover the contents of the bucket which, all the same, I associate with the bureaucrat's astounding suggestion.

IX

'And one has nothing and nobody, and one travels about the world with a trunk and a case of books, and really without curiosity. What sort of a life is it really, without a house, without inherited possessions, without dogs?'

Sometimes I think that the author of those words must have been under a sentence not unlike mine.

It may seem incredible that such a man, a writer of genius and famous into the bargain, could have been found guilty of any crime. But the hard and incomprehensible fact stands that the most frequent convictions and the heaviest sentences fall to the lot of just such sensitive, intelligent individuals as this very poet whose words have so much emotional significance for me. There is, I believe, a kind of telepathy between the condemned, a sort of intuitive recognition which can even make itself felt through the medium of the printed page. How else should I feel – without fear of appearing presumptuous, either – for this great man of another nation, this dead man whom I never saw and to whom I could not have spoken, the tender, wincing, pathetic solicitude that painfully comes into being only between fellow sufferers? How intimately I experience in my heart just what he must have felt in all of those unknown rooms, some of them poor, perhaps, and some splendid, but all opposing him with the cold fearful indifference of other people's belongings, against which he has to defend himself as best he can with his poor lonely trunk and his case of books.

And I – I haven't even a case of books to defend me. In my defence I can call up only the few volumes for which I was able to make room when the clothes and personal necessities had been packed into my trunk. They are honourable and precious to me, these books, in proportion to their great heroism. They are like members of a suicide squad who do not hesitate to engage the enormously superior enemy, life, upon my behalf.

When I start to think of my books individually it is always the same one which takes first place in my mind: the only one of the bodyguard about whose loyalty, so to speak, I have any doubt. I have had this book that I'm thinking of for a long time, and until just lately it has never been out of my keeping. I'm not sure how it reached me originally, whether it was a present or whether I came across it by accident on some bookseller's shelves. I only know that the author's name was unfamiliar to me. I read it first during that fabulously remote period before my troubles began. I remember the horror the story inspired in me then and how I wondered that any normal brain could conceive and elaborate so dreadful a theme.

But then, as things went from bad to worse with me, as my circumstances became more and more unpropitious, as I wandered further and further into the maze of misfortune from which I have never succeeded in extricating myself, then my feelings towards the book underwent a change.

How can I describe the profoundly disturbing suspicion that slowly grew upon me, for which at the start there was no sort of justi-fication? Again and again I tried to rid myself of it. But like a latent venom it dwelt obstinately in my blood, poisoning me with the idea that the story told in the book related to myself, that I myself was identified in some obscure way with the principal character. Yes, in time it crystallized into this: the terrible book revealed itself as my manual, tracing the path I was doomed to tread, step by step, to the lamentable and shameful end.

If I had come to detest the book it would have been natural. If I had destroyed it or thrown it away one could have understood that. But instead I developed a curious attachment to it, a dependence upon it which is very hard to explain. Of course, there were times when I reacted against the book. On such occasions I felt convinced that it was the origin of my bad luck and that all the disasters which have overtaken me would never have happened had I not first read about them in its pages. But then, immediately afterwards, I would be eagerly turning those pages to discover what fresh tragic or humiliating or confusing experience was lying ahead of me.

This ambivalent attitude prevented me from coming to any hard-and-fast decision about the book, but whether I regarded it as an evil omen or as a talisman, it was always of the greatest significance to me, and the idea of parting from it was unthinkable. I even felt uneasy if I was separated from it for more than a few hours. Particularly on those days which I expected to bring forth some new development in my case, a superstitious anxiety compelled me to carry the book everywhere I went.

That was how I came to be carrying it under my arm in the adviser's office. How I wish now that I had left it at home. But how could I possibly have guessed that I should be required to deposit some item of personal property there as a token? It came as the greatest surprise to me when, at the end of the interview, I was informed of this regulation. And why did this adviser select the book as a suitable object, drawing it from under my arm with a smile and putting it down on the top of a pile of other books on a writing desk in the corner? He might just as well have taken my scarf or one of my gloves or even my watch. I have wondered since then why I didn't make any protest. But at the time I allowed him to take the book from me without a word. I was too disconcerted to think clearly, and I was unsure of myself. I was afraid of prejudicing myself in the eyes of the man upon whose somewhat doubtful advice I was prepared to rely. Once he had taken the book in his curiously small, delicate hands it was too late to interfere.

But each time I go into the room and see it lying there, inaccessible although within easy reach, a conflict begins in my heart and I feel deeply disturbed. I start wondering whether my wisest course would not be to seize the book and carry it off, even at the cost of forgoing a support which, however dubious, is all that's left to me now.

X

My new adviser does not understand my case. There, now I have written the words I knew all the time I would have to write sooner or later. I am not surprised. Not at all. It would have been a thousand times more surprising if he, who is not even a native of our city, could have found his way through the enormously intricate labyrinth which a case that's been going on as long as mine has is bound to become. The thing which does surprise me is my own optimism. Surely I ought to recognize now that my number is up. Where do I always find enough courage for one more last hope? I am the enemy of this indestructible, pitiless hope which prolongs and intensifies all my pain. I would like to lay hold of hope and strangle it once and for all.

I have been to the adviser's office today. It is in a large building full of offices. To get to it from the street I had to walk up an alleyway between barbed wire and concrete-filled bins placed there to impede an attacking force. The officials who work in this building have a vast clientele. You can hardly pass through the alley without danger of being pushed into the barbed wire by one of the people who must hurry to get in or out of the place as quickly as possible. They are preoccupied individuals who frown incessantly, and the king himself would have to step briskly aside, if some abstracted client lost in anxiety took the notion of rushing past headlong to an appointment. It is noticeable that nearly all these impetuous, worried creatures are carrying briefcases of varying sizes which one can presume to contain the most urgent secret documents, the most dramatic dossiers. But I also saw commonplace people coming and going, little men with umbrellas hooked on their arms and women with shopping bags full of parcels.

The waiting-room, when I finally got there, was crowded with people I seemed to have seen somewhere else. Yes, I already seemed to know all their faces only too well. When I had taken the vacant chair that might have been left purposely for me, I saw that among them, as they sat restlessly fidgeting, there were several boys and girls, schoolchildren and some even younger. Although I'm not particularly fond of children I couldn't help pitying the poor little things, growing up in the vile atmosphere all these rooms have, impregnated with fear and suspense. What could they be but innocent at their early age? And what sort of future could be in store for lives beginning so inauspiciously? But the children themselves paid no attention to their environment. The youngest ones slept on their mother's laps: Some of the others leaned with empty faces against the knees or shoulders of grown-up people. Some were bored and made quiet overtures to each other to pass the time. A boy in a leather jacket had climbed on the window-sill; he had got his paper-white forehead pressed to the pane and was gazing out at the sky as if saying goodbye to it. In a far corner of the room, two big men whose shoulders carried the words 'Heavy Rescue' had spread themselves out in chairs and were staring dolefully at their huge black boots projecting in front of them. The air was stale, torpid, laden with unquiet breaths.

Meanwhile a constant bustle was going on in other parts of the building: one heard footsteps hurrying about, boards creaking, doors opening and closing, voices raised sometimes in question or argument. Only we in the waiting-room seemed shut off from participation in the activity, like forgotten castaways wrecked in some stagnant lagoon.

From time to time the door opened a little way and an indistinctly seen person peeped in and beckoned to one of the waiting clients who immediately jumped up and rushed out as if at the point of a bayonet. A stir of excitement went through the room each time this occurred, and it would be some minutes before those who were left behind settled down again to their restless vigil. I don't know how long this went on. I have the impression that hours passed, perhaps half a day. While I waited I remembered the important man who had been my adviser in former times; his elegant town house, his major-domo, the room with wine-coloured curtains where he used to receive me so promptly. The fact that I now had to seek advice in such a humble and undignified fashion brought home to me painfully how my affairs had changed for the worse. It was as if the authorities, by sending me here, had set their official seal on my degradation.

At last it was my turn to receive the mysterious summons. I had decided that when it came I would walk calmly across the room without impatience or flurry, but, just like everyone else, I found myself jumping up and making a dash for the door as if my life depended on getting through it at lightning speed. It was so dark in the corridor that I could only dimly distinguish a man's figure walking ahead of me with nonchalant steps. He opened a door on the left, signalled me to enter and followed me in. Apparently it was the adviser himself who had come for me. He was a young, rather plump man, a foreigner obviously, with an impeccably tied bow tie, and there was about him that finical, even dainty air which stout people sometimes have. It was the tie in particular which gave this effect, as if a neat, blue-spotted butterfly had alighted under his chin.

He stood fingering the ends of the bow delicately for a moment, smiling at me in a way that was both absent-minded and polite, before he invited me to sit down. I took the chair that he indicated and began to explain my case. The room was quite small and square, with green walls. Outside the window, almost touching the glass, was a large tree still covered, in spite of the lateness of the season, with trembling green leaves. As the leaves stirred, watery shadows wavered over the ceiling and walls, so that one had the impression of being enclosed in a tank.

I felt singularly uncomfortable. My case was difficult to describe. I did not know where to start or which particulars to relate, which to omit, since it was clearly impossible to mention every detail of the enormously protracted and complex business.

The young foreigner sat listening to me without making a single note. His manner was perfectly correct, but I somehow had the impression that he was not fully attentive. I wondered how much he understood of what I was saying: it was clear to me from the few words he had spoken that his grasp of the language was far from perfect. And why did he not write down at least some of the salient points of my statement? He surely didn't propose to rely purely on memory in such a complicated affair? Now and then he fingered the wings of his tie and smiled absently, but whether at me or at his own thoughts there was no way of knowing.

The situation suddenly appeared heartbreaking, futile, and I felt on the verge of tears. What was I doing here in this tank-like room, relating my private and piercing griefs to a smiling stranger who spoke in a different tongue? I thought I should stand up and go away, but I heard myself talking in agitation, begging him to realize the extreme gravity of my predicament and to give it more serious consideration, seeing that he was my last available source of assistance.

The young adviser smiled at me politely and made some vague fluttering movements with his small hands, at the same time saying a few words to the effect that my case was not really so exceptional as I thought; that it was, in fact, quite a common one. I protested that he must be mistaken, perhaps had not understood me completely. He smiled again and repeated those indeterminate motions which possibly were intended to be reassuring but which only conveyed to me a distrustful sense of misapprehension. Then he glanced at his watch in a way that was meant to signify the end of the interview and instructed me to come back again in two or three days.

I don't remember how I got out of the building. I've no recollection of passing between the coils of barbed wire in the alley. The sun was setting, and I was in a residential part of the city that was strange to me. I walked up long, hilly, deserted streets between large houses, most of which seemed to be uninhabited. Dry autumnal weeds grew tall in the gardens, and the black window holes gaped with jagged fringes like mirror fragments in which the last rays of the sun stared at themselves bitterly. Then I passed a stranger who glanced coldly at me, and other strangers passed by with cold faces, and still other strangers. Armoured vehicles, eccentrically coloured, stood in an endless chain at the roadside, painted with cabbalistic signs. But what these symbols meant I had no idea. I had no idea if there were a place anywhere to which I could go to escape from the strangeness, or what I could do to bear being a stranger in our strange city, or whether I should ever visit that stranger who was my adviser again.

A BRIGHT GREEN FIELD

IN MY TRAVELS I am always being confronted by a particular field. It seems that I simply can't escape it. Any journey, no matter where it begins, is apt to end towards evening in sight of this meadow, which is quite small, sloping and in the vicinity of tall dark trees.

The meadow is always beautifully green; in the dusk it looks almost incandescent, almost a source of light, as though the blades of grass themselves radiated brightness. The vividness of the grass is always what strikes people first; it takes them a moment longer to notice that, as a matter of fact, the green is rather too intense to be pleasant and to wonder why they did not see this before. The observation once made, it becomes obvious that for grass to be luminiferous is somewhat improper. It has no business to advertise itself so ostentatiously. Such effulgent lustre is unsuited to its humble place in the natural order and shows that in this meadow the grass has risen above itself – grown arrogant, aggressive, too full of strength.

Its almost sensational, inappropriate brightness is always the same. Instead of changing with the seasons, as if to underline the insolence of the grass, the field's brilliance remains constant, although in other ways its aspect varies with the time and place. It is true that, besides being always bright green, the field is always small, always sloping, always near big dark trees. But size and colour are relative; different people mean different things when they speak of a small bright meadow or a big dark tree. The idea of a slope is flexible, too, and, although a persistent divergence from the horizontal is characteristic of the field, the degree of steepness fluctuates widely.

The slant may be imperceptible, so that one would swear the surface was as flat as a billiard table. There have been times when I couldn't believe – until it was proved to me by measurements taken with a clinometer – that the ground was not perfectly level. On other occasions, in contrast with what may be called an invisible incline, the meadow appears to rise almost vertically.

I shall never forget seeing it so that thundery summer day, when, since early morning, I had been travelling across a great dusty plain. The train was oppressively hot, the landscape monotonous and without colour, and, during the afternoon, I fell into an uneasy doze from which I woke to the pleasant surprise of seeing mountain slopes covered with pines and boulders. But, after the first moment, I found that, with the mountains shutting out the sky, the enclosed atmosphere of the deep ravine was just as oppressive as that of the flat country. Everything looked drab and dingy, the rocks a nondescript mottled tint, the pines the shiny blackish-green of some immensely old shabby black garment – their dense foliage, at its brightest the colour of verdigris, suggesting rot and decay, had the unmoving rigidity of a metal with the property of absorbing light and seemed to extinguish any occasional sunbeam that penetrated the heavy clouds. Although the line kept twisting and turning, the scenery never changed, always composed of the same eternal pine forest and masses of rock, pervaded, as the plain had been, by an air of dull, sterile monotony and vegetative indifference.

The train suddenly wound around another sharp bend and came out into a more open place where the gorge widened, and I saw, straight ahead, between two cataracts of black trees, the sheer emerald wall that was the meadow, rising perpendicular, blazing with jewel-brightness, all the more resplendent for its dismal setting.

After the dim monochrome vistas at which I had been looking all day, this sudden unexpected flare of brilliance was so dazzling that I could not immediately identify the curious dark shapes dotted about the field, still further irradiated, as it was now, by the glow of the setting sun, which broke through the clouds just as I reached the end of my journey, making each blade of grass scintillate like a green flame.

The field was still in full view when I emerged from the station, a spectacular vivid background to the little town, of which it appeared to be an important feature, the various buildings having been kept low and grouped as if to avoid hiding it. Now that I was able to look more carefully, and without the distorting and distracting effect of the train's motion, I recognized the peculiar scattered shapes I had already noticed as prone half-naked human bodies, spreadeagled on the glistening bright green wall of grass. They were bound to it by an arrangement of ropes and pulleys that slowly drew them across its surface and had semi-circular implements of some sort fastened to their hands, which they continually jerked in a spasmodic fashion, reminding me of struggling flies caught in a spider's web. This tormented jerking, and the fact that the grotesque sprawling figures were chained to the tackle pulling them along, made me think they must be those of malefactors undergoing some strange archaic form of punishment conducted in public up there on the burning green field. In this, however, I was mistaken.

A passer-by presently noticed my interest in the mysterious movements outlined so dramatically on the brilliant green and, seeing that I was a stranger, very civilly started a conversation, informing me that I was not watching criminals, as I had supposed, but labourers engaged in cutting the grass, which grew excessively fast and strongly in that particular field.

I was surprised that such a barbarous mowing process should be employed merely to keep down the grass in a small field, even though, in a way, it formed part of the town, and I inquired whether their obviously painful exertions did not jeopardize the health and efficiency of the workers.

Yes, I was told, unfortunately the limbs, and even the lives, of the men up there were in danger, both from the effects of overstrain and because the securing apparatus was not infrequently broken by the violence of their muscular contractions. It was regrettable, but no alternative method of mowing had so far been discovered, since the acute angle of the ground prohibited standing upon it or even crawling across on all fours, as had at times been attempted. Of course, every reasonable precaution was taken; but, in any case, these labourers were expendable, coming from the lowest ranks of the unskilled population. I should not pay too much attention to the spasms and convulsions I was observing, as these were mainly just mimicry, a traditional miming of the sufferings endured by earlier generations of workers before the introduction of the present system. The work was now much less arduous than it looked and performed under the most humane conditions that had as yet been devised. It might interest me to know that it was not at all unpopular; on the contrary, there was considerable competition for this form of employment, which entailed special privileges and prestige. In the event of a fatality, a generous grant was made to the dependants of the victim, who, in accordance with tradition, was always interred *in situ* – a custom dating from antiquity and conferring additional prestige, which extended to the whole family of the deceased.

All this information was given in a brisk, matter-of-fact way that was reassuring. But I could not help feeling a trifle uneasy as I gazed at the meadow, compelled by a kind of grisly fascination to watch those twitching marionettes, dehumanized by the intervening distance and by their own extraordinary contortions. It seemed to me that these became more tortured as the sun went down, as though a frantic haste inspired the wild uncoordinated swinging of the sickles, while the green of the grass brightened almost to phosphorescence against the dusk.

I wanted to ask why the field had to be mown at all – what would it matter if the grass grew long? How had the decision to cut it been made in the first place all those years ago? But I hesitated to ask questions about a tradition so ancient and well established; evidently taken for granted by everyone, it surely must have some sound rational basis I had overlooked – I was afraid of appearing dense or imperceptive or lacking in understanding – or so I thought. Anyhow, I hesitated until it was too late, and my informant, suddenly seeming to notice the fading light, excusing himself, hurried on his way, barely giving me time to thank him for his politeness.

Left alone, I continued to stand in the empty street, staring up, not quite at ease in my mind. The stranger's receding steps had just ceased to be audible when I realized that I had refrained from asking my questions, not for fear of appearing stupid but because, in some part of me, I already seemed to know the answers. This discovery distracted me for the moment; and when, a few seconds later, my attention returned to the field, the row of jerking puppets had vanished.

Still I did not move on. An apathetic mood of vague melancholy had descended on me, as it often does at this hour of the changeover from day to night. The town all at once seemed peculiarly deserted and quiet, as though everyone were indoors, attending some meeting I knew nothing about. Above the roofs, the mountain loomed, gloomy, with pines flowing down to the hidden gorge, from several parts of which evening mist had begun to rise, obscuring my view of the slopes but not of the meadow, still vividly green and distinct.

All at once I found myself listening to the intense stillness, aware of some suspense in the ominous hush of impending thunder. Not a sound came from anywhere. There was no sign of life in the street, where the lights had not yet come on, in spite of the gathering shadows. Already the houses around me had lost their sharp outlines and seemed huddled together, as if nervously watching and waiting and holding their breath. Mist and twilight had blotted out colours, all shapes were blurred and indefinite, so that the clear-cut bright green field stood out startlingly, mysteriously retaining the light of the departed day concentrated in its small rectangle, floating over the roofs like a bright green flag.

Everywhere else, the invisible armies of night were assembling, massing against the houses, collecting in blacker blackness beneath the black trees. Everything was waiting breathlessly for the night to fall. But the advance of darkness was halted, stopped dead, at the edge of the meadow, arrested by sheer force of that ardent green. I expected the night to attack, to rush the meadow, to overrun it. But nothing happened. Only, I felt the tension of countless grass blades, poised in pure opposition to the invading dark. And now, in a first faint glimmer of understanding, I began to see how enormously powerful the grass up there must be, able to interrupt night's immemorial progress. Thinking of what I'd heard, I could imagine that grass might grow arrogant and far too strong, nourished as this had been; its horrid life battening on putrescence, bursting out in hundreds, thousands, of strong new blades for every single one cut.

I had a vision then of those teeming blades – blades innumerable, millions on millions of blades of grass – ceaselessly multiplying, with unnatural strength forcing their silent irresistible upward way through the earth, increasing a thousand-fold with each passing minute. How fiercely they crowded into that one small field, grown unnaturally strong and destructive, destruction-fed. Turgid with life, the countless millions of blades were packed densely together, standing ready, like lances, like thickets, like trees, to resist invasion.

In the midst of the deep dusk that was almost darkness, the brilliance of that small green space appeared unnatural, uncanny. I had been staring at it so long that it seemed to start vibrating, pulsating, as if, even at this distance, the tremendous life surge quickening it were actually visible. Not only the dark was threatened by all that savage vitality; in my vision I saw the field always alert, continually on the watch for a momentary slackening of the effort to check its growth, only awaiting that opportunity to burst all bounds. I saw the grass rear up like a great green grave, swollen by the corruption it had consumed, sweeping over all boundaries, spreading in all directions, destroying all other life, covering the whole world with a bright green pall beneath which life would perish. That poison-green had to be fought, fought; cut back, cut down; daily, hourly, at any cost. There was no other defence against the mad proliferation of grass blades, no other alternative to grass, blood-bloated, grown viciously strong, poisonous and vindictive, a virulent plague that would smother everything, everywhere, until grass and grass only covered the face of the globe.

It seems monstrous, a thing that should never have been possible, for grass to possess such power. It is against all the laws of nature that grass should threaten the life of the planet. How could a plant meant to creep, to be crushed underfoot, grow so arrogant, so destructive? At times the whole idea seems preposterous, absolutely crazy, a story for children, not to be taken seriously – I refuse to believe it. And yet . . . and yet . . . one can't be quite certain . . . Who knows what may have happened in the remote past? Perhaps, in the ancient archives kept secret from us, some incident is recorded . . . Or, still further back, before records even began, something may have deviated from the norm . . . Some variation, of which nothing is known any more, could have let loose on the future this green threat.

One simply doesn't know what to believe. If it is all just a fantasy, why should I have seen, as in a vision, that grass, fed on the lives of bound victims, could become a threat to all life, death-swollen and horribly strong? In the beginning, when the whole thing started, did the threat come before the victim or vice versa? Or did both evolve simultaneously out of a mutual need for one another? And how do I come into it? Why should I be implicated at all? It's nothing to do with me. There's nothing whatever that I can do. Yet this thing that should never have happened seems something I cannot escape. If not today or tomorrow, then the day after that, or the next, at the end of some journey one evening, I shall see the bright green field waiting for me again. As I always do.

ICE STORM

I WENT TO CONNECTICUT on a Wednesday morning by the eleven-thirty train. It was snowing in New York,

FREAK STORM ICES AND SOAKS CITY BY TURNS TIES TRAFFIC

but Grand Central Station was cosy thick amber winter warmth. I always did like Grand Central. It was the first place I got to recognize when I first came to New York, and in those frightening days I used to orientate myself by it in my journeys about the city. Grand Central wasn't gloomy like a London station, nor awe-inspiring like a cathedral, nor frivolous like a theatre; nor was it purely functional. There was a sort of generalized serviceable brightness about it which bolstered up my belief that a rational existence might still be possible somewhere, despite all evidence to the contrary.

I hired a redcap to carry my bag, although it was not especially heavy. Having my bag carried made me feel extravagant. I had the idea that the extravagance was justified in view of the situation. The situation was bad. I had to make an important decision which in itself was a hard thing for me to do, and whichever way I decided the result was bound to be bad. I had to decide whether to continue the struggle with life in America or whether to throw my hand in and start struggling all over again on some other continent. I was going to Connecticut to make the decision because I hoped that I might be able to think more impersonally and calmly in the country. In New York I could not concentrate on anything at all.

ICY GOING ON THE SKYWAY

I couldn't concentrate long enough even to read a paper in New York City.

The redcap found me a seat in the coach and put my bag on the rack, and the train started off three minutes late by my old wristwatch from Basle.

I sat and looked at the back of the seat in front of me. Green-blue, peacock-blue plush, with a metal band running along the top. The white ticket, eighty-five-cents'-worth of travelling, stuck under the metal band. In England only the first-class tickets were white. No classes here. Just Pullman and coaches. Democracy. Democracy of the democrats. By the democrats. For the democrats. The train went faster. Democracy; democracy; democracy. We ran over some points. Democ, democ, democ.

After a while I looked out of the window. Instead of the blue plush, houses, the electric snake sliding insidiously between gaunt buildings with fire escapes. Then a cemetery. The country opening. A frozen grey pond untidily scuffed with white and hobbledehoy charging figures crouched low over sticks. Black grasses bristling out of whiteness. Festoons of dirtyish ice hung from rocks like soiled cotton wool. A smug antiseptic-looking gargantuan face, every girl's magazine cover college boyfriend, magnified to the nth degree and thanking God he's American. I began to feel cold and lonely

CARS HAD TOUGH GOING ON THE PULASKI YESTERDAY

and turned back to the blue plush and submerged myself in stuffy train overheat. Sink. Drown that decision.

The train was slowing down now. I felt the decision bubble to the top of my mind. Gassy bubbles of anxiety bursting through the steam-heated stupefied daze.

AS FREAK NORTHEASTER COVERED ROADWAY WITH
SHEET OF ICE

No, I don't want to think about the decision yet. I put on my fur coat and fastened it carefully and tied my scarf and opened my handbag. Looking at myself in the glass, the eyes looked slightly bloodshot and my face had bad lines under the make-up. Suddenly I began to feel lonely again; a bitter loneliness was making my throat stiffen. God, life is hell when you've lost your security, your background.

GREY BLACK CRANE OR HERON WINGS ICED
FORCED TO EARTH ALONG WATERFRONT

Is it possible that this is really happening to me?

PEOPLE WERE SURPRISED AT THE WEATHER

A jolt, cold air coming in, the handle of the suitcase sharp in the palm of my hand.

On the platform the cold flared stark up against my face. I held myself taut and walked straight at it. There was hardly any snow here. Only a neat white line accenting one side of things. Everything looked frozen steel-hard. Metallic hardness bleakly trapped the station buildings. Nothing but grey ice in the sky.

The Drakes had driven in to meet me. Gloria looked pinched. Her heart-shaped, small-featured, flattish face made me think of a small pretty snake caught by the frost. She had on a pair of red corduroy pants and a blue woollen hood with a pompom behind. She gave me a vinegary kind of smile when she said hello. Al looked fine in his checked hunting cap. His brown eyes were bright like a healthy dog's.

'You look as if living in the country suited you,' I said to him.

'You bet it suits me,' he said, grinning. 'It's a swell life.'

'The city for me, thank you,' Gloria said, sourly sweet.

We got into the car and drove down the main street. Gloria wanted to go to a movie. She said, 'You can hardly prise me out of the house this weather, but once I am out I like to do something just to make sure I'm still alive. I might forget otherwise.'

The movie theatre didn't open till two thirty. There was an hour to wait. We went into a drugstore to eat. Nobody wanted any of the food that was there. We ate bacon and tomato sandwiches, and a draught came in every time the door opened, and every time this happened Gloria shivered and pursed up her narrow red lips and just did not make a hissing sound. She kept talking about how cold it was in the country and how you might just as well be buried alive as living in that neck of the woods where they were. I was trying to keep my mind off the decision I had to make, off the minutes ducking under the hands of the clock over the counter. 'I can't imagine', Gloria said to me, 'why you should want to come down here when you've got a nice warm Manhattan apartment.'

Finally it was time to go. The cold outside was something unnatural.

COUNTRY SLAPPED IN THE FACE BY BEAUTIFYING
YET MOST DESTRUCTIVE RAIN SLEET AND SNOWSTORMS
CITIZENS HAVE SEEN SINCE NOTORIOUS ICING OF

It seemed to come at one in a steady stream the way ultra-violet rays come out of a doctor's lamp. The houses looked wizened and shrunk into themselves. It was too cold to think of anything in the street.

For the first few seconds after we got inside, the warmth of the movie theatre was like heaven. To be warm seemed to be all anyone could possibly ask of the world. I saw my reflection hanging in the blank glare of a mirror across the vestibule and noticed the dark lines around my eyes and mouth. Gosh, I thought to myself, what a wreck I've turned into lately. New York life is certainly hard to take.

The picture was about the North-West Mounted Police, and it

included a great deal of blood and some waving of flags. Now you can have a good time feeling sentimental every time you see the Union Jack, Gloria said. She had a way of speaking that made everything she said seem like a small delicate snake darting its tongue at you.

When she made that remark I stopped following the activities of the North-West Mounted Police and began to think about England, about how I felt about England, if I did feel at all. I remembered a few days back noticing a Rolls-Royce parked by the St Regis and walking around to see if it had a GB plate on the back and feeling happy because it had. I didn't pay any attention to this incident when it occurred, but recalling it now in the stuffy darkness it struck me as one of the saddest things that had ever happened, a thing almost too pathetic to be endured. It seemed to me to be one of those incidents which, if you happened to see them objectively, would practically break your heart.

STORM-NUMBED PIGEON FOUND WITH FEET FROZEN
TO PARK BENCH AT 62ND STREET AND CENTRAL PARK WEST

I thought I'd already experienced every possible degree of cold, but driving in the dark to the Drakes' house it was colder still. Gloria was all right in her trousers and fur-lined boots, but I sat and froze in my town clothes. I sat huddled upon the back seat. There was no rug. In five minutes my legs started to feel numb. I bent down and rubbed my ankles through the smooth cold-feeling nylon stockings. Frost kept clouding the windshield faster than the wipers could clear it away. Al drove slowly, skidding on the icy places. In a way I was glad of the cold because it was far too cold to think about anything.

By the time we got to the house I could hardly get out of the car, I was so stiff with cold.

WHEN AL LEVINE RETURNED TO HIS CAR ON
EAST 42ND STREET IT LOOKED LIKE A FROZEN DESSERT

The black sky sagged like a doom over our heads. Suddenly something began to fall out of the sky. Arrows seemed to be falling out of the blackness. While it was in the air it seemed to be long shafts of rain falling down, but as soon as it touched anything it was ice. The sting of it on your face was like whips.

'Jesus, there's going to be an ice storm,' Al said. 'You two dames get inside while I lock up the car.'

Gloria and I ran for the house, and the interminable evening began. We had supper and played some records and sat about. The Drakes' kid played on the floor and made a considerable noise. It was impossible to think. Gloria kept darting her little forked questions at me, wanting to find out what was wrong.

'I'm thinking of leaving the States,' I told her.

'What would you want to do that for?' she asked.

'I don't seem able to cope with life here,' I said.

'You've done mighty well for yourself, if you ask me,' Al said. 'You started cold not long ago, and now you've earned some dough and got fixed up in a swell apartment and made a whole lot of friends. Jesus, what more do you want?'

'You're spoiled, that's the trouble with you,' Gloria said. 'You've always been over-privileged. You don't know what it is to be really broke like we were when we first came to New York. You haven't got what it takes to see a thing through unless all the advantages are handed out to you on a plate.'

'Living alone in a foreign country is what gets me down,' I said.

'I don't understand you,' Gloria said. 'If you really feel as badly as you say, how can you be so articulate about everything and write about everything the way you do?'

Al's dumb animal's eyes were looking at me.

'There's something in that about being on your own,' he said in his slow way. 'With Gloria and me now, even when it was tough sledding, we were always a unit. Being broke, well, that was tough. But in a way it wasn't really tough, because as soon as we got a few bucks I used to go out and buy the biggest goddam beefsteak I could find, and we'd cook it up for ourselves and then we'd be all right.'

'She's got Charles backing her,' Gloria said.

'Not any more,' I said.

'He'll always let you have money even if he won't see you,' she said.

'Money isn't everything,' I said.

UNEXPECTED SLEETSTORM HITS CITY
CAUSES SCORES OF ACCIDENTS AND

'It's the hell of a long way towards everything,' Gloria said.

I got up rather quickly and looked out of the window. It was hot in the room, but there was a fringe of long icy tears suspended outside the window.

KEEPS AMBULANCES BUSY DAY AND NIGHT

God damn your self-pity, I said to myself.

'Oh, I've got no sympathy for you,' Gloria said.

The evening went on and on. Every now and then Al went to look out. He always came back saying the storm was still going on. We got through the time somehow and went to bed.

In the morning the world had changed into the weirdest and most awful thing I had ever seen. The world was new and difficult to believe. The ice was not falling out of the sky any more, but everything in the world was loaded with ice. Every tree was bowed down with ice, huge branches and here and there whole trees had broken with the weight of ice that encased every twig in a thick and transparent shell.

After breakfast I put on the warmest clothes I could find and went out into that awful desolation. There was no glitter about the ice because the sun did not shine. The sky was still grey and bitter; a heavy mist blocked the end of every perspective like a grey curtain. Absolute stillness. Negation of everything.

It was not easy to walk on the frozen road.

This loneliness, I thought, is my loneliness. I was the only person out in the glacial world. I touched an ice-coffined briar with my hand, and it snapped off, more brittle than a Venetian vase.

I walked on clumsily, slipping on the ice now and then. The big unbroken trees sprayed like unclear fountains towards the mist. Through the centre of each jet of clouded crystal the black branch was threaded. The trees were lovely and frightening to look at. I tried not to feel afraid of the trees. Dear God, let me not start being afraid of things in the natural world. It's only the human world that is truly fearful.

Most of the telegraph wires were broken, and every wire was encased in about four inches of solid ice. The icy casing of the telegraph wires was toothed like the rows of spikes that are put on the tops of walls to keep people from climbing over, only these spikes pointed downwards. Occasionally a yard or more of the frozen armature would fall from one of the wires which had not given way, and when this happened the crash of the splintering ice on the iron ice of the road was sudden and terrifying like a bomb bursting into the silence.

I came to a plantation of pine trees, each tree bending a different way as if meditating alone. Every pine needle was rigid in ice, and the bowed and bristling trees looked like the arched necks of dragons, of dinosaurs. They were very fantastic-looking shapes. Fantastic and lonely.

Well, I thought, whatever happens I'll have seen a good deal of what goes on in different places. I've certainly been getting around lately. Six times across the equator and a typhoon off Cuba and now an ice storm in Connecticut.

I spent most of the day looking at the appalling and beautiful spectacle of Connecticut under the ice. I felt less bad while I was walking about.

MANAGER OF MAYFLOWER HOTEL DRUGSTORE PLAYS
NURSE TO PIGEON FOUND HALF FROZEN ON PARK BENCH

When it got dark the temperature rose, and the ice started to melt. I had hoped that the frost would hold so that it would be impossible to drive to the station and I should be able to go on walking about the country feeling less and less bad until I was capable of making a reasoned decision.

But when I heard in the night the slow heavy slither of ice on the roof and the rumbling crash as it fell I knew I should have to go back to New York.

The next day Al drove me to the station. The ice was turning to slush on the roads. The trees were all black again. Except that I had seen the ice storm everything was exactly the same for me as it had been in all the days of my indecision.

From the train window I looked at the ruined strangeness, the mess of ice

CITY SLOSHES OUT OF SLEET

in the streets.

It was much too hot in the train. I sat there and was carried back to New York. I didn't think about anything much or try to decide anything. It seemed to me that I might as well leave everything to chance. Because there were far too many decisions to make about everything and no permanent set of values by which to decide.

ALL SAINTS

Le Toussaint.

Why should there be rats in a new white villa with blue shutters and the Cinzano advertisement? The new house rather narrow and tall like a white shoebox set up on end, the windows symmetrical in front with their blue shutters and the blank side wall painted entirely blue, yellow Cinzano prancing slantwise across. Beautiful blue, blank blue, sky colour, Mary's colour, blue colour shining with brightness because of the loveliness of our sweet Lady.

But nobody honours the Virgin any more. Only the little girls walking in new white and junket faces to first communion, and not in meditation at that. The Lady is withdrawn, in her blue gown, on the other side of the candles out of which burgeons the brand-new Renault of M. Fortunat.

Let the blueness of the blank wall atone. Let the blue wall atone for what withdraws on the other side. The wirehaired terrier with rickets, brought from the city in a basket to lie in the sunshine, *chien de race* and worth several thousand francs, several thousand francs worth of hair and bone dying on the small iron balcony between the shutters.

Can the rats see through a blue wall? Do they see those who are there dissembling and the love about to be proffered to oblivion with the dying dog and the red cups white spotted like toadstools and the powdered glass in the Armagnac when the neck of the bottle was broken?

What was that noise like an egg breaking?

an egg breaking

why? and who broke? and where?

Not thrown exactly, not accidentally let fall. Dropped through slotted light and shadow to break on stone, the smooth egg, the symbol (one said, Nirvana is egg-shaped), the complete thing. And then the impact, smashing, the yellow disintegration. A cold tongue of the Haute Tech licked the yolk off the rock. Dying by proxy, the consumptive girl, whose life connects with nothing but a thermometer, has dropped into the stream the egg which it was not permitted to leave on the breakfast tray.

That prize the rat dragging his slimy belly in the long grass loses; needing, however, only a little patience for something much more substantial.

What is this? what are you saying? you never say what you are saying.

I'm saying that it's November and they are selling chrysanthemums, white chrysanthemums for the dead.

I never like white flowers, they remind me of funerals . . . Mr and Mrs Who sit sincerely thank . . . beautiful floral tributes . . . recent sad bereavement . . . O for the grip of a vanished hand and the sound of a voice that . . .

In the Lexington undertaking parlour there was a coffin lined with white satin and the cutest little white satin pillow inside with ruffled edges and everything . . .

but right in the window like that with everyone who passed looking at it, it hardly seemed . . .

casket, not coffin, dear . . .

the price included the hire of a dozen gilt chairs, and candles, too, electric presumably . . .

they rouge the cheeks and use lipstick so that you'd never know . . . eau-de-Cologne as well . . . no expense spared . . . it's wonderful how they think of everything these days.

In all the graveyards the bitter smell of chrysanthemums. Wearing black stockings and crêpe bands and viscerally oppressed by greasy déjeuner processes, the mourners disconsolately loiter through the dank afternoon between jimcrack contraptions of beads and twisted wire commemorating their departed relations. Damp clay clings premonitorily to their boot soles. The smell of rotting vegetation titillates the rheum in their nostrils. Among the soggy stunted leaves of the chrysanthemums decomposition has already set in. Fog drapes clammily the bare chestnut branches, and through the sour slime of the decaying leaves a rat is stealthily sliding.

What has the rat got to do with it? Must we keep thinking about rats?

What else should we think about?

the end of every project comes down to the rat.

Certainly it must have found its way under the white serge of that mourner and eaten away the heart if ever there was one . . .

don't look now, but she's there again, ghastlier than ever, and the dogs are just bags of bones.

There she goes up the slope to the cemetery with her white serge costume, skeleton lank, and the violet powder on her crêpey cheeks, and the terrible gash of lipstick like heart disease.

On leashes she holds the two dogs which, but for these sustaining thongs, seem likely to fall down, brittle legs too weak to carry even such an insignificant weight of emaciation . . .

they're thinner every day, I swear they are . . . and those sores . . . it oughtn't to be allowed.

At the gate she pauses. Her long black Lillie Langtry lady-like shoes fastidiously squelch the mire churned up by bourgeois footgear. Claw within lisle glove, one hand tentatively scrabbles the ironwork in a fashion suggestive of exploratory familiarity with the interiors of dustbins.

But just imagine white serge in November . . . imagine white serge at any time . . . must be about a 1900 model . . . people oughtn't to be allowed to make such scarecrows of themselves . . . ought to have more consideration for others . . . disgusting really . . . and those dogs . . . they ought to be put out of their misery . . . why doesn't somebody do something about it?

She's reached her destination, she's got her hand on the knob, everything seems to be working to a conclusion. But there's that last-minute hitch. Something's missing after all. What is it that's not there? What's lacking underneath the white serge?

Most unfortunate, profoundly desolating, but really, you know, nothing can be done without it, it's absolutely essential to produce it before any action can be taken . . . you say the rat? . . . my dear madame, I'm extremely sorry, inconsolable, in fact . . . but there's simply no provision made . . . it's not as if one could do anything oneself either . . .

With lisle fingers she smooths a droplet from the end of her nose, examines briefly the damp smear, puts into stiff motion the stilt-like mechanism of her lower limbs. Feebly submissive, the dogs totter alongside.

Don't look now, but she's going . . . the dogs can hardly drag one foot after the other . . . it's a disgrace . . . cruelty to dumb animals . . . why does she always come as far as this gate and then go away . . . staring in like that . . . ghoulish I call it . . .

don't look now, but she's got the scrubbiest little bit of fur you ever saw around her neck . . . looks just like a dead rat . . . don't look now . . . don't look . . .

THE OLD ADDRESS

THE DAY SISTER COMES in while I'm packing to leave. She's about ten feet tall and, as if to disguise the fact, usually adopts a slouch and keeps her hands in her pockets under the starched apron. Now, however, she has a big envelope marked Patient's Property in one hand, which she holds out to me.

'You won't need this, but we have to return it to you now you're being discharged.'

I take it. How very odd. I get a sensation like dreaming as I feel through the paper the familiar barrel-shape of the syringe I haven't felt for so long.

'It's no use anyhow', I say to her, 'without something to put in it.' This doesn't sound quite the right thing, so I add, 'I may as well leave it here', and drop it nonchalantly into the wastepaper basket.

She stares at me so hard that I wonder what's in her mind. Finally she shrugs her shoulders and slouches out, omitting to say goodbye.

I wait until I'm sure she's not coming back, then retrieve the envelope and put it into my bag. I've no particular object in doing so; the action seems pretty well automatic. I sit down to wait for someone to come and fetch me, but I'm too restless to keep still, so I put my coat on and walk out of the ward and along a passage, past a number of people, none of whom takes the slightest notice of me.

Besides the syringe, the usual collection of things, including money, is in my bag. If anybody asks questions, I'm on my way to buy farewell presents for the nurses. Commendable, surely?

No questions are asked. The porter shoves the revolving door. I go down the steps of the main entrance and on to the pavement.

I'm outside again. Free. Also, of course, I'm still guilty and always shall be. I don't feel anything much, though, except that it's strange to be out here on my own. After a few steps strange equates with disturbing. This isn't the world I know. I look all around, at the crowds, the skyscrapers, the mass of traffic. It all looks delirious, ominous, mad.

There's an absolute mob surging along the pavement; you can't move without bumping into someone. I search in vain for a human face. Only hordes of masks, dummies, zombies go charging past, blindly, heads down. Stern condemnatory faces of magistrates glare at me from their pedestals at street corners. Cold enemy eyes, arrow eyes, pierce me with poison-tipped suspicion, as if they know where I've come from.

Terrible eyes. Terrible noise. Terrible traffic.

The sky is full of unnatural light, which is really a darkish murk and makes everything look sinister, a black conspiracy hanging up there in the air. Something frightful seems to be happening or going to happen.

The traffic roars, bellows, hurls itself in a torrential surge as into battle – cars thresh about like primeval monsters. Some have grins of diabolical joy on their malevolent rudimentary faces, gloating over prospective victims. They're anticipating the moment when their murderous deadweight of hard heavy metal will tear into soft, vulnerable, defenceless flesh, mashing it into a pulp, which, thinly spread on the roadway, creates a treacherous slippery surface where other cars skid in circles, their wheels entangled in sausage-strings of entrails bursting out of the mess.

Suddenly I notice that one car has selected me as its prey and is making straight for me through all the chaos. Come on then! Knock me down, run over me, cut off my existence. I don't want it – don't like it. I never did. The size of a locomotive, the hideous great mechanical dinosaur bears down upon me. Already the metal assassin towers over my head.

And now the dingy mass hits me with the full force of its horrid inhuman horsepower, a ton or so of old iron to finish me off. I'm demolished, done for, down on the pavement which is already black with my blood. Lying there, mangled, splintered, a smashed matchbox, all at once I find I'm transformed into an inexhaustible fountain, spouting blood like a whale.

Huge black clots, gouts, of whale blood shoot high in the air, then splash down in the mounting flood, soaking the nearest pedestrians. Everybody is slipping and slithering, wading in blood. It's over their ankles. Now it's up to their knees. All along the street, children start screaming, licking blood off their chins, tasting it on their tongues just before they drown.

The grown-ups can't save them; they're drowning, too. Fine! Splendid! Let them all drown, the bastards; they've all done their best to destroy me. I hate them all. There's no end to my blood supply. It's been turned on full at the main, at high pressure; nobody knows how to turn it off. Everywhere people are coughing and choking, their lungs are filling with my unbreathable blood, and it's poison, a deadly poison, to them.

Wonderful! At last I'm being revenged on those who have persecuted me all my life. I've always loathed the horrible hostile creatures pressing around me in a suffocating mass, trying to get me down, to trample on me. Down with them now! Now it's their turn to suffocate. I laugh in their faces, smeared and streaked like Red Indians with my blood. And all the time my broken thorax goes on pouring out blood.

They're out of their depth now. They try to swim. But their clothes are too heavy, already saturated by the thick, sticky, steaming tide. Inevitably, they are dragged under, writhing, shouting and struggling. Wasting their strength in idiotic contortions, they're all sinking and drowning already. I lash out wildly at the few survivors, hit them as hard as I can, bash them on the head, forcing them down into the sea of blood as if they were so many eels. Down, wantons, down!

Suddenly the show's over. Sudden lightning strikes overhead. A forked tree of blinding brilliance flares up the sky, setting fire to it as it goes. In a flash, the whole sky is a sheet of flame, consumed, gone up in smoke. Nothing is left where the sky used to be except an expanse of grimy canvas like the walls of a tent. No wonder the light's unnatural and things look strange, when the city, and most likely the whole world, is imprisoned under this gigantic tent, cut off from the sun, moon and stars.

Why did I ever imagine that I was free? The truth is I couldn't be more thoroughly trapped. Those vast walls enclosing me in an unbroken circle have now assumed a more spectral aspect and look more like mist. But this doesn't make them any less impenetrable, impassable. Not at all. Only too well I know that there's no way through them, that I shall never escape.

The thought of being shut in for ever drives me out of my senses, so that I try to bash down walls with my bare hands, tear at bricks with my nails, pick the mortar out. It's too ghastly. I'm not the sort of person who can live without seeing the sky. On the contrary, I have to look at it many times a day; I'm dying to be a part of it like the stars themselves. A cold finger of claustrophobia touches me icily. I can't be imprisoned like this. Somehow or other I must get out.

Suddenly on the edge of panic, I look around desperately for help. But, of course, I'm alone, as I always am. The pavements are deserted; there isn't a soul in sight. Once again I've been betrayed and abandoned; by the whole human race this time. Only the traffic continues to hurtle past, cascades of cars racing along the street in a ceaseless metallic flood.

Above the din of their engines, louder crashes erupt all around. Avalanches of deafening noise explode in my ears like bombs. In all the thunderous booming roar I can distinguish the sobs of heartbroken children, the shrieks of tortured victims and addicts deprived of drugs, sadistic laughter, moronic cries, the moans of unsuccessful suicides – the whole catastrophe of this inhuman city, where the wolf-howl of ambulances and police cars rises perpetually from dark gullies between the enormous buildings.

Why am I locked in this nightmare of violence, isolation and cruelty? Since the universe only exists in my mind, I must have created the place, loathsome, foul as it is. I live alone in my mind, and alone I'm being crushed to suffocation, immured by the walls I have made. It's unbearable. I can't possibly live in this terrible, hideous, revolting creation of mine.

I can't die in it either, apparently. Demented, in utter frenzy, I rush madly up and down, hurl myself like a maniac into the traffic, bang my head with all my force against walls. Nothing changes. It makes no difference. The horror goes on just the same. It was enough that the world seemed to me vile and hateful for it to be so. And so it will remain, until I see it in a more favourable light – which means never.

So there's to be no end to my incarceration in this abominable, disgusting world . . . My thoughts go round in circles. Mad with despair, I don't know what I'm doing, I can't remember or think any more. The terror of life imprisonment stupefies me; I feel it inside me like an intolerable pain. I only know that I must escape from this hell of hallucination and horror. I can't endure my atrocious prison a moment longer.

There's only one way of escape that I've ever discovered, and needless to say I haven't forgotten that.

So now I wave my arm frantically at a passing taxi, fall inside and tell the man to drive to the old address.

A VISIT

ONE HOT NIGHT A leopard came into my room and lay down on the bed beside me. I was half asleep and did not realize at first that it was a leopard. I seemed to be dreaming the sound of some large, soft-footed creature padding quietly through the house, the doors of which were wide open because of the intense heat. It was almost too dark to see the lithe, muscular shape coming into my room, treading softly on velvet paws, coming straight to the bed without hesitation, as if perfectly familiar with its position. A light spring, then warm breath on my arm, on my neck and shoulder, as the visitor sniffed me before lying down. It was not until later, when moonlight entering through the window revealed an abstract spotted design, that I recognized the form of an unusually large, handsome leopard stretched out beside me.

His breathing was deep although almost inaudible; he seemed to be sound asleep. I watched the regular contractions and expansions of the deep chest, admired the elegant relaxed body and supple limbs and was confirmed in my conviction that the leopard is the most beautiful of all wild animals. In this particular specimen I noticed something singularly human about the formation of the skull, which was domed rather than flattened, as is generally the case with the big cats, suggesting the possibility of superior brain development inside. While I observed him, I was all the time breathing his natural odour, a wild primeval smell of sunshine, freedom, moon and crushed leaves, combined with the cool freshness of the spotted hide, still damp with the midnight moisture of jungle plants. I found this non-human scent, surrounding him like an aura of strangeness, peculiarly attractive and stimulating.

My bed, like the walls of the house, was made of palm leaf matting stretched over stout bamboos, smooth and cool to the touch, even in the great heat. It was not so much a bed as a room within a room, an open staging about twelve feet square, so there was ample space for the leopard as well as myself. I slept better that night than I had since the hot weather started, and he, too, seemed to sleep peacefully at my side. The close proximity of this powerful body of another species gave me a pleasant sensation I am at a loss to name.

When I awoke in the faint light of dawn, with the parrots screeching outside, he had already got up and left the room. Looking out, I saw him standing, statuesque, in front of the house on the small strip of ground I keep cleared between it and the jungle. I thought he was contemplating departure, but I dressed and went out, and he was still there, inspecting the fringe of the dense vegetation in which huge heavy hornbills were noisily flapping about.

I called him and fed him with some meat I had in the house. I hoped he would speak, tell me why he had come and what he wanted of me. But although he looked at me thoughtfully with his large lustrous eyes, seeming to understand what I said, he did not answer but remained silent all day. I must emphasize that there was no hint of obstinacy or hostility in his silence, and I did not resent it. On the contrary, I respected him for his reserve; and, as the silence continued unbroken, I gave up expecting to hear his voice. I was glad of the pretext for using mine and went on talking to him. He always appeared to listen and understand me.

The leopard was absent during much of the day. I assumed that he went hunting for his natural food; but he usually came back at intervals and seldom seemed to be far away. It was difficult to see him among the trees, even when he was quite close, the pattern of his protective spots blended so perfectly with the pattern of sunspots through savage branches. Only by staring with concentrated attention could I distinguish him from his background; he would be crouching there in a deep-shaded glade or lying extended with extraordinary grace along a limb of one of the giant kowikawas, whose branch structure supports less robust trees as well as countless creepers and smaller growths. The odd thing was that, as soon as I'd seen him, he invariably turned his head as if conscious that I was watching. Once I saw him much further off, on the beach, which is only just visible from my house. He was standing darkly outlined against the water, gazing out to sea; but even at this distance, his head turned in my direction, although I couldn't possibly have been in his range of vision. Sometimes he would suddenly come indoors and silently go all through the house at a quick trot, unexpectedly entering one room after another, before he left again with the same mysterious abruptness. At other times he would lie just inside or outside with his head resting on the threshold, motionless except for his watchful moving eyes and the twitching of his sensitive nostrils in response to stimuli which my less acute senses could not perceive.

His movements were always silent, graceful, dignified, sure, and his large, dark eyes never failed to acknowledge me whenever we met in our daily comings and goings.

I was delighted with my visitor, whose silence did not conceal his awareness of me. If I walked through the jungle to visit someone or to buy food from the neighbouring village, he would appear from nowhere and walk beside me but always stopped before a house was in sight, never allowing himself to be seen. Every night, of course, he slept on the bed at my side. As the weeks passed he seemed to be spending more time with me during the day, sitting or lying near me while I was working, now and then coming close to gaze attentively at what I was doing.

Then, without warning, he suddenly left me. This was how it happened. The rainy season had come, bringing cooler weather; there was a chill in the early-morning air when he returned to my room as I finished dressing and leaned against me for a moment. He had hardly ever touched me in daylight, certainly never in that deliberate fashion. I took it to mean that he wished me to do something for him and asked what it was. Silently he led the way out of the house, pausing to look back every few steps to see whether I was coming, and into the jungle. The stormy sky was heavily clouded; it was almost dark under the trees, from which great drops of last night's rain splashed coldly on my neck and bare arms. As he evidently wanted me to accompany him further, I said I would go back for a coat.

However, he seemed to be too impatient to wait, lunging forward with long, loping strides, his shoulders thrusting like steel pistons under the velvet coat, while I reluctantly followed. Torrential rain began streaming down; in five minutes the ground was a bog into which my feet sank at each step. By now I was shivering, soaked to the skin, so I stopped and told him I couldn't go on any further. He turned his head and for a long moment his limpid eyes looked at me fixedly with an expression I could not read. Then the beautiful head turned away, the muscles slid and bunched beneath patterned fur, as he launched himself in a tremendous leap through the shining curtain of raindrops, and was instantly hidden from sight. I walked home as fast as I could and changed into dry clothes. I did not expect to see him again before evening, but he did not come back at all.

Nothing of any interest took place after the leopard's visit. My life resumed its former routine of work and trivial happenings. The rains came to an end, winter merged imperceptibly into spring. I took pleasure in the sun and the natural world. I felt sure the leopard meant to return and often looked out for him, but throughout this period he never appeared. When the sky hung pure and cloudless over the jungle, many-coloured orchids began to flower on the trees. I went to see one or two people I knew; a few people visited me in my house. The leopard was never mentioned in our conversations.

The heat increased day by day; each day dawned glassily clear. The atmosphere was pervaded by the aphrodisiac perfume of wild white jasmine, which the girls wove into wreaths for their necks and hair. I painted some large new murals on the walls of my house and started to make a terrace from a mosaic of coloured shells. For months I'd been expecting to see the leopard, but as time kept passing without a sign of him I was gradually losing hope.

The season of oppressive heat came around in due course, and the house was left open all night. More than at any other time, it was at night, just before falling asleep, that I thought of the leopard, and, although I no longer believed it would happen, pretended that I'd wake to find him beside me again. The heat deprived me of energy; the progress of the mosaic was slow. I had never tried my hand at such work before, and, being unable to calculate the total quantity of shells that would be required, I constantly ran out of supplies and had to make tiring trips to the beach for more.

One day while I was on the shore, I saw, out to sea, a young man coming towards the land, standing upright on the crest of a huge breaker, his red cloak blowing out in the wind, and a string of pelicans solemnly flapping in line behind him. It was so odd to see this stranger with his weird escort, approaching alone from the ocean on which no ships ever sailed, that my thoughts immediately connected him with the leopard: there must be some contact between them; perhaps he was bringing me news. As he got nearer, I shouted to him, called out greetings and questions, to which he replied. But because of the noise of the waves and the distance between us, I could not understand him. Instead of coming on to the beach to speak to me, he suddenly turned and was swept out to sea again, disappearing in clouds of spray. I was puzzled and disappointed. But I took the shells home, went on working as usual and presently forgot the encounter.

Some time later, coming home at sunset, I was reminded of the young man of the sea by the sight of a pelican perched on the highest point of my roof. Its presence surprised me: pelicans did not leave the shore as a rule; I had never known one come as far inland as this. It suddenly struck me that the bird must be something to do with the leopard, perhaps bringing a message from him. To entice it closer, I found a small fish in the kitchen, which I put on the grass. The pelican swooped down at once, and with remarkable speed and neatness, considering its bulk, skewered the fish on its beak, and flew off with it. I called out, strained my eyes to follow its flight, but only caught a glimpse of the great wings flapping away from me over the jungle trees before the sudden black curtain of tropical darkness came down with a rush.

Despite this inconclusive end to the episode, it revived my hope of seeing the leopard again. But there were no further developments of any description; nothing else in the least unusual occurred.

It was still the season when the earth sweltered under a simmering sky. In the afternoons the welcome trade wind blew through the rooms and cooled them, but as soon as it died down the house felt hotter than ever. Hitherto I had always derived a nostalgic pleasure from recalling my visitor; but now the memory aroused more sadness than joy, as I had finally lost all hope of his coming back.

At last the mosaic was finished and looked quite impressive, a noble animal with a fine spotted coat and a human head gazing proudly from the centre of the design. I decided it needed to be enclosed in a border of yellow shells and made another expedition to the beach, where the sun's power was intensified by the glare off the bright-green waves, sparkling as if they'd been sprinkled all over with diamonds. A hot wind whistled through my hair, blew the sand about and lashed the sea into crashing breakers, above which flocks of sea birds flew screaming, in glistening clouds of spray. After searching for shells for a while I straightened up, feeling almost dizzy with the heat and the effort. It was at this moment, when I was dazzled by the violent colours and the terrific glare, that the young man I'd already seen reappeared like a mirage, the red of his flying cloak vibrating against the vivid emerald-green waves. This time, through a haze of shimmering brilliance, I saw that the leopard was with him, majestic and larger than life, moving as gracefully as if the waves were solid glass.

I called to him, and, although he couldn't have heard me above the thundering of the surf, he turned his splendid head and gave me a long, strange, portentous look, just as he had that last time in the jungle, sparkling rainbows of spray now taking the place of rain. I hurried towards the edge of the water, then suddenly stopped, intimidated by the colossal size of the giant rollers towering over me. I'm not a strong swimmer; it seemed insane to challenge those enormous oncoming walls of water, which would certainly hurl me back contemptuously on to the shore with all my bones broken. Their exploding roar deafened me, I was half blinded by the salt spray; the whole beach was a swirling, glittering dazzle in which I lost sight of the two sea-borne shapes. And when my eyes brought them back into focus, they had changed direction, turned from the land and were already a long way off, receding fast, diminishing every second, reduced to vanishing point by the hard, blinding brilliance of sun and waves.

Long after they'd disappeared, I stood there, staring out at that turbulent sea on which I had never once seen any kind of boat and which now looked emptier, lonelier and more desolate than ever before. I was paralysed by depression and disappointment and could hardly force myself to pick up the shells I'd collected and carry them home.

That was the last time I saw the leopard. I've heard nothing of him since that day or of the young man. For a little while I used to question the villagers who lived by the sea; some of them said they vaguely remembered a man in a red cloak riding the water. But they always ended by becoming evasive, uncertain and making contradictory statements, so that I knew I was wasting my time.

I've never said a word about the leopard to anyone. It would be difficult to describe him to these simple people who can never have seen a creature even remotely like him, living here in the wilds as they do, far from zoos, circuses, cinemas and television. No Carnivora, no large or ferocious beasts of any sort have ever inhabited this part of the world, which is why we can leave our houses open all night without fear.

The uneventful course of my life continues; nothing happens to break the monotony of the days. Some time, I suppose, I may forget the leopard's visit. As it is I seldom think of him, except at night when I'm waiting for sleep to come. But, very occasionally, he still enters my dreams, which disturbs me and makes me feel restless and sad. Although I never remember the dreams when I wake, for days afterwards they seem to weigh me down with the obscure bitterness of a loss which should have been prevented and for which I am myself to blame.

FOG

I ALWAYS LIKED TO drive fast. But I wasn't driving as fast as usual that day, partly because it was foggy but mainly because I felt calmly contented and peaceful, and there was no need to rush. The feeling was injected, of course. But it also seemed to have something to do with the fog and the windscreen wipers. I was alone, but the swinging wipers were keeping me company and acting as tranquillizers as they cleared their half-circles of glass, helping me to feel not quite there, as if I was driving the car in my sleep. The fog helped, too, by blurring the world outside the windows so that it looked vague and unreal.

These people looked as unreal as everything else. I'd just driven over a level crossing when they appeared ahead, a group of long-haired, exotically dressed teenagers, laughing and talking and singing as they wandered along hand in hand or with arms around each other's waists, all of them obviously on top of the world. In the ordinary way it would have annoyed me to see them straggling all over the road as if they owned it. I would have resented their being so sure of themselves, so relaxed and gay, when I often felt depressed, insecure and lonely and had no one to talk to or laugh with. But this lot couldn't disturb me because they weren't real. I remained perfectly cool and detached, even though they didn't attempt to get out of the way and actually signalled to me to stop.

I just looked indifferently at their silly faces surrounded by all that idiotic hair in wet snake-like strands, every grinning face wet and glistening with fog, every mouth opening and shutting with breath steaming out of it in clouds. They reminded me of Japanese dragon-masks and also of the subhuman nightmare mask-faces in some of Ensor's paintings. These faces grimacing at me through the fog had the same sort of slightly eerie repulsiveness of masks, of walking and talking things, not really alive. They'd have repelled me if they'd been human beings. But as they were only dummies I felt nothing about them, my indifference was unaffected. It was just that I would have preferred not to be looking at them.

I had no intention of giving any of them a lift, naturally. However, as they wouldn't get off the road, I automatically moved my foot from the accelerator towards the brake. But then I thought, why? They weren't real. None of this was real. I wasn't really here, so they couldn't be either. It was absurd to treat them as real live people. So back went my foot on to the accelerator again. They were just a collection of disagreeable masks I was looking at in my sleep. I was absolutely detached and cool; there wasn't a trace of emotion involved, no feeling whatever.

One dummy came up too close to me. Through the fog, I saw the painted mask-face opposite mine, staring straight at me, mouth and eyes opening wider and wider in a grotesque caricature of incredu-lity. Then there was a bump, and I gripped the wheel hard with both hands as if this was what had to be done to avert some disaster – precisely what disaster seemed immaterial.

The incident was unduly prolonged. Strange caterwaulings went on interminably and indistinct shapes fell about. When at last it was over, I drove on as if nothing had happened. Nothing had really. I didn't give it a thought; there was nothing to think about. I just went on driving calmly and carefully in the fog, the windscreen wipers swinging regularly to and fro, promoting that peaceful dream-like sense of not being present.

An abrupt apparition loomed up at a foggy corner, slewed right across the road. The idea of avoiding a crash between our two unrealities never entered my head: some reflex action must have made me swerve at the last moment and scrape past a huge articulated lorry. Ignoring the driver's shouts, I drove on again, doing thirty-five to forty, not more, not thinking of anything in particular, the wipers swinging, the fog making everything vague.

It was pleasantly soothing to feel so detached, so tranquil. Then it began to get boring. Everything went on and on: the fog, the windscreen wipers, my driving. It was as if I didn't know how to stop the car and would have to drive till the tank was dry or all roads came to an end.

So I was quite relieved when the police car stopped me. I got out and stood in the road and asked what they wanted. They could see for themselves that I wasn't drunk, and I certainly hadn't been driving dangerously. A sergeant asked me to come to the station, and I agreed. It was all the same to me where I was, as I wasn't there really. I might as well be at a police station as anywhere else. They wanted to search the car, and I made no objection. There was nothing to be found in it; the syringe and the rest of the stuff was in my bag. While I was waiting for them to finish I looked out of the window. It was dusk now outside. I watched the lights come on and shine yellow in the foggy street.

An inspector interviewed me alone in a small, cold, brightly lit room with notices in small print on the walls and two bicycles leaning against them. We sat on hard wooden chairs on opposite sides of a desk covered in black Formica. I kept my coat collar turned up. He was a big man whose very square shoulders somehow looked artificial. I thought of those dummies children make with coat-hangers and sticks and cushions stuffed inside clothes. His face was an imitation, a mask made of cardboard or papier mâché with green eyes painted on. In the strong light I saw these eyes watching me vacuously, without any expression, gazing blankly at my hair, my watch, my suede coat.

I looked back at them calmly, indifferently, wondering what they were seeing, if anything. Obviously he wasn't real. He was just a sham,

I was seeing him in my sleep, so he couldn't disturb me. That was all I was thinking. I was absolutely cool and detached, there wasn't a trace of emotion involved, not even when he asked if I'd witnessed the accident at the level crossing.

The room was so cold that his breath steamed out in front of him while he was speaking. For a second I seemed to be watching the steaming mouths of those other masks, bobbing about in the fog like horrid Hallowe'en pumpkins with candles smoking inside. His boring proletarian face looked unreal and subhuman like theirs. He had the same slightly weird repulsiveness of a talking thing, not in any way human. He would have repelled me if he'd been real. But he was only a dummy, an ersatz man, so he couldn't affect my detachment any more than they could. I felt nothing whatever about him. I was indifferent. It was just that I'd have preferred not to be sitting there facing him. I said, 'No, I didn't see anything.' I had no intention of telling him, naturally. Not that there was anything to tell. None of this was real. It couldn't really be happening.

'You may be able to help us in our investigations.'

I didn't know what to say to this, so I remained silent. How could I possibly help if I hadn't seen what took place? He felt in one pocket, then in another, brought out a packet of Player's and offered it to me. His hands were big, square, used-looking, like a working man's. 'No thanks. I don't smoke.' I sniffed with distaste the strong, rather stale smell of the Virginian tobacco.

'What, no vices?' He almost smiled, momentarily; I wondered why. He was pretending, putting on some sort of act. I looked indifferently, silently, at his mass-produced nonentity's face. There was no gleam of light, no life, in his eyes, they were flat green stones, devoid of intelligence or expression. I leaned my elbows on the desk. The situation was prolonging itself unduly. It had become boring. I looked at my watch.

A policewoman brought in a tray, put it down on the desk and went out again. I took the thick white cup the inspector held out to me and drank some of the tea, or it might have been coffee. The fog was starting to make my throat slightly sore.

'Do you want one of these?' I looked from his artisan's hands to the plate of plain dry biscuits and shook my head. He took one himself, broke it in half and swallowed it in two mouthfuls. I put the white cup down on the desk.

He said, 'Someone has been killed at the level crossing.'

Three deep horizontal frown lines appeared on his forehead. His eyes were screwed up and half shut. For a second I again saw the teenage masks floating about in the fog. One came too close and looked me straight in the face with a ludicrously exaggerated expression of amazement or disbelief. The mask-face across the desk was frowning at me. I knew he was waiting for me to say something, but there was nothing to say. A mask had been put out of circulation. So what? A mask wasn't human. It was meaningless, unimportant. The whole thing was unreal.

He had refilled his cup; steam was rising from it. Through the steam, his stereotyped imitation face floated in front of me as if in fog, the green eyes, now wide open, staring straight at me, but blankly, perhaps unseeing, they looked almost blind. His square shoulders loomed through the fog; he was a dummy made of stuffed clothes and umbrellas, not real. Since he wasn't a human being I could look at him without feeling, with perfect indifference. It was just that I didn't want to look at him. I turned my head.

The fog was thickening outside as evening came on. I felt the rawness of it in my throat. Outside the window, fog pressed closely against the glass. For a second I felt trapped in a cold cell surrounded by fog. But I wasn't here really. Nothing about the situation was real, so the room couldn't be. The solid look of the walls was an illusion; in reality they consisted of empty space, a field of force between particles in a boundless void. Still, I would have preferred to be somewhere else.

I still felt peaceful, but now I'd begun to be dimly aware of some distant threat to peace. I put it out of my mind as I heard him say, 'Think! Are you quite sure you saw nothing unusual on the road? No one who'd been injured?'

'I've told you, I didn't see anything at all.'

'But the lorry driver says you passed him directly after the accident. So surely you must have seen something.'

His voice sounded sharper. I had the idea that he glanced at me sharply, almost as if he was really alive. But when my eyes got back to him the mask was the same, with the eyes half shut again as before, painted flat on the frowning fake-face.

'What lorry driver?' I asked. 'I don't know what you're talking about. Can't you see it's all a mistake and I'm not the person you want?'

I looked at my watch again. He hadn't answered me. I watched him start looking through a small notebook in a shiny black cover. I was still coolly indifferent, insulated by detachment. But a disturbing doubt was creeping in somewhere. It was beginning to seem as if the situation might never end at all: and I wasn't entirely sure my detachment would last out an interminable situation. Watching him turn the pages of the small book, I was again aware of a far-off threat, a black cloud on a remote horizon.

'The driver took the car's registration number.' He had found what he wanted and now read out some figures to me. 'That's the number of your car, isn't it? So you see there can't be any mistake. And it is you we want.' He moved abruptly, leaned right over the desk, bringing his face so near mine that instinctively I drew back from the smell of stale smoke and infrequently cleaned heavy clothes, mixed with a faint sharper, sicklier smell of alcohol.

'Suppose you start telling me the truth now.' The tone of his voice was surprisingly new and peremptory. His empty, expressionless eyes had suddenly come to life. His dull dummy-policeman's face looked unexpectedly real and threatening.

I could feel the black cloud coming closer as I watched him get up and walk around the desk, his gaze and movements now permeated by a chilly deliberation. He stood over me ominously, his big, square, worker's hands right in my line of vision, yellowish against the dark uniform, ominously powerful; his padded-looking shoulders bending slightly, ominously, towards me – and much too close. I didn't want to see him. I looked around him, out of the window, instead.

I could smell the fog, I could taste it, it rasped my throat. Outside, daylight was going fast. The street was completely deserted. I heard no traffic noises from other streets. A low, dirty, foggy ceiling pressed down from above, dingily reflecting the lights of the town. The fog itself was thicker than ever and had turned a dense, bilious yellow, like vomit. The window-panes failed to keep it out of the room. Horizontal lines of fog hung visibly in the air; the lights shone dull yellow through them.

For a moment I felt trapped again, this time by something darker and deadlier than the fog. I still wasn't quite there. But my injected tranquillity was gradually wearing off, and, even without being fully identified with the situation, it was becoming difficult to ignore the existence of some sort of threat somewhere. I suspected that I was about to lose my detachment, and then everything would become intolerable.

So, after all, this did somehow concern me, although I couldn't see how, on account of the fog. The fog was everywhere; it was inside my head. I seemed not to understand quite what had been happening . . . not to remember . . . it was as if I didn't quite grasp what was going on. I had the impression of having lost touch, lost control of events, while all the time a black cloud of something like poison gas was surging towards me.

I suddenly wanted to escape then, before it was too late. I knew I must take immediate action to extricate myself from the situation. But I couldn't do this as long as things seemed unreal and I wasn't really here, so first I had to stop feeling absent and disconnected. All of a sudden, I urgently wanted to wake up, not just sit here in my sleep but be really here, instead of nowhere.

However, it seemed to be too late already. I saw that there was no escape from the situation. The black cloud filled the room; I was breathing in poison as well as fog, inhaling a poisonous mixture of stale smoke and alcohol smell.

Then I looked around and instantaneously stopped wanting to wake up. The last thing I wanted was to be awake here, when I saw the inspector still standing horribly close, no longer a lifeless dummy, a commonplace cardboard mask, but a sinister human being with frightening powers over me, whose green watching eyes had turned cold, ruthless, piercing, in a hard face now ominously alive and real, accusatory, unmistakably menacing.

All I wanted then was for everything to go on as before, so that I could stay deeply asleep and be no more than a hole in space, not here or anywhere at all, for as long as possible, preferably for ever.

WORLD OF HEROES

I TRY NOT TO look at the stars. I can't bear to see them. They make me remember the time when I used to look at them and think, I'm alive, I'm in love and I'm loved. I only really lived that part of my life. I don't feel alive now. I don't love the stars. They never loved me. I wish they wouldn't remind me of being loved.

I was slow in starting to live at all. It wasn't my fault. If there had ever been any kindness I would not have suffered from a delayed maturity. If so much apprehension had not been instilled into me, I shouldn't have been terrified to leave my solitary unwanted childhood in case something still worse was waiting ahead. However, there was no kindness. The nearest approach to it was being allowed to sit on the back seats of the big cars my mother drove about in with her different admirers. This was, in fact, no kindness at all. I was taken along to lend an air of respectability. The two in front never looked around or paid the slightest attention to me, and I took no notice of them. I sat for hours and hours and for hundreds of miles inventing endless fantasies at the back of large and expensive cars.

The frightful slowness of a child's time. The interminable years of inferiority and struggling to win a kind word that is never spoken. The torment of self-accusation, thinking one must be to blame. The bitterness of longed-for affection bestowed on indifferent strangers. What future could have been worse? What could have been done to me to make me afraid to grow up out of such a childhood?

Later on, when I saw things more in proportion, I was always afraid of falling back into that ghastly black isolation of an uncomprehending, solitary, over-sensitive child, the worst fate I could imagine.

My mother disliked and despised me for being a girl. From her I got the idea that men were a superior breed, the free, the fortunate, the splendid, the strong. My small adolescent adventures and timid experiments with boys who occasionally gave me rides on the backs of their motorbikes confirmed this. All heroes were automatically masculine. Men are kinder than women; they could afford to be. They were also fierce, unpredictable, dangerous animals: one had to be constantly on guard against them.

My feeling for high-powered cars presumably came from my mother, too. Periodically, ever since I can remember, the craving has come over me to drive and drive, from one country to another, in a fast car. Hearing people talk about danger and death on the roads seems ludicrous, laughable. To me, a big car is a very safe refuge and the only means of escape from all the ferocious cruel forces lurking in life and in human beings. Its metal body surrounds me like magic armour, inside which I'm invulnerable. Everybody I meet in the outside world treats me in the same contemptuous, heartless way, discrediting what I do, refusing to admit my existence. Only the man in the car is different. Even the first time I drive with him, I feel that he appreciates, understands me; I know I can make him love me. The car is a small speeding substitute world, just big enough for us both. A sense of intimacy is generated, a bond created between us. At once I start to love him a little. Occasionally it's the car I love first: the car can attract me to the man. When we are driving together, the three of us form one unit. We grow into each other. I forget about loneliness and inferiority. I feel fine.

In the outside world catastrophe always threatens. The news is always bad. Life tears into one like a mad rocket off course. The only hope of escaping is in a racing car.

At last I reached the age of freedom and was considered adult, but still my over-prolonged adolescence made me look less than my age.

X, a young American with a 2.6-litre Alfa Romeo and lots of money, took me for fifteen or sixteen. When I told him I was twenty-one he burst out laughing, called me a case of retarded development, seemed to be making fun of me in a cruel way. I was frightened, ran away from him, travelled around with some so-called friends with whom I was hopelessly bored. After knowing X, they seemed insufferably dull, mediocre, conventional. Obsessed by longing for him and his car, I sent a telegram asking him to meet us. As soon as I'd done it, I grew feverish with excitement and dread, finally felt convinced the message would be ignored. How idiotic to invite such a crushing rejection. I should never survive the disappointment and shame.

I was shaking all over when we got to the place. It was evening. I hid in the shadows, kept my eyes down so as not to see him – not to see that he wasn't there. Then he was coming towards us. He shook hands with the others one by one, leaving me to the last. I thought, he wants to humiliate me. He's no more interested in me than he is in them. Utterly miserable, I wanted to rush off and lose myself in the dark. Suddenly he said my name, said he was driving me to another town, said goodbye to the rest so abruptly that they seemed to stand there, suspended, amazed, for the instant before I forgot their existence. He had taken hold of my arm and was walking me rapidly to his car. He installed me in the huge, docile, captivating machine, and we shot away, the stars spinning loops of white fire all over the sky as we raced along the deserted roads.

That was how it began. I always think gratefully of X, who introduced me to the world of heroes.

The racetrack justifies tendencies and behaviour which would be condemned as antisocial in other circumstances. Risks encountered nowhere else but in war are a commonplace of the racing drivers' existence. Knowing they may be killed any day, they live in a wartime atmosphere of recklessness, camaraderie and heightened perception. The contrast of their light-hearted audacity and their sombre, sinister, menacing background gave them a personal glamour I found irresistible. They were all attractive to me, heroes, the bravest men in the world. Vaguely, I realized that they were also psychopaths, misfits, who played with death because they'd been unable to come to terms with life in the world. Their games could only end badly: few of them survived more than a few years. They were finished, anyhow, at thirty-five, when their reactions began to slow down, disqualifying them for the one thing they did so outstandingly well. They preferred to die before this happened.

Whether they lived or died, tragedy was waiting for them, only just around the corner, and the fact that they had so little time added to their attraction. It also united them in a peculiar, almost metaphysical way, as though something of all of them was in each individual. I thought of them as a sort of brotherhood, dedicated to their fatal profession of speed.

They all knew one another, met frequently, often lived in the same hotels. Their life was strictly nomadic. None of them had, or wanted to have, a place of his own to live in, even temporarily, far less a permanent home. The demands of their work made any kind of settled existence impossible. Only a few got married, and these marriages always came unstuck very quickly. The wives were jealous of the group feeling; they could not stand the strain, the eternal separation, the homelessness.

I had never had a home, and, like the drivers, never wanted one. But wherever I stayed with them was my proper place, and I felt at home there. All my complicated emotions were shut inside hotel rooms, like boxes inside larger ones. A door, a window, a looking-glass, impersonal walls. The door and the window opened only on things that had become unreal, the mirror only revealed myself. I felt protected, shut away from the world as I was in a car, safe in my retreat.

Although, after winning a race, they became for a short time objects of adulation and public acclaim, these men were not popular; the rest of humanity did not understand them. Their clannishness, their flippant remarks and casual manners were considered insulting; their unconventional conduct judged as immoral. The world seemed not to see either the careless elegance that appealed to me or their strict aristocratic code, based on absolute loyalty to each other, absolute professional integrity, absolute fearlessness.

I loved them for being somehow above and apart from the general gregarious mass of mankind, born adventurers, with a breezy disrespect for authority. Perhaps they felt I was another misfit, a rebel, too. Or perhaps they were intrigued or amused by the odd combination of my excessively youthful appearance and wholly pessimistic intelligence. At all events, they received me as no other social group could ever have done – conventions, families, finances would have prevented it. Straight away they accepted my presence among them as perfectly natural, adopted me as a sort of mascot. They were regarded as wild, irresponsible daredevils, but they were the only people I'd ever trusted. I was sure that, unlike all the others I'd known, they would not let me down.

Their code prohibited jealousy or any bad feeling. Unpleasant emotional situations did not arise. Finding that I was safe among them, I perceived that it was unnecessary to be on my guard any longer. Their attitude was at the same time flattering and matter-of-fact. They were considerate without any elaborate chivalry, which would have embarrassed me, and they displayed a frank, if restrained, physical interest, quite willing, apparently, to love me for as long or short a time as I liked. When my affair with A was finally over, I simply got into B's car, and that was that. It all seemed exceedingly simple and civilized.

The situation was perfect for me. They gave me what I had always wanted but never had: a background, true friends. They were kind in their unsentimental racetrack way, treated me as one of themselves, shared with me their life histories and their cynical jokes, listened to me with attention but did not press me to talk. I sewed on buttons for them, checked hotel and garage accounts, acted as unskilled mechanic, looked after them if they were injured in crashes or caught influenza.

At last I felt wanted, valued, as I'd longed to be all my life. At last I belonged somewhere, had a place, was some use in the world. For the very first time I understood the meaning of happiness, and it was easy for me to be truly in love with each of them. I could hardly believe I wasn't dreaming. It was incredible; but it was true, it was really happening. I never had time now to think or to get depressed, I was always in a car with one of them. I went on all the long rallies, won Grand Prix races, acted as co-driver or passenger as the occasion required. I loved it all: the speed, the exhaustion, the danger. I loved rushing down icy roads at ninety miles an hour, spinning around three times and continuing non-stop without even touching the banked-up snow.

This was the one beautiful period of my life, when I drove all over the world, saw all its countries. The affection of these men, who risked their lives so casually, made me feel gay and wonderfully alive, and I adored them for it. By liking me, they had made the impossible happen. I was living a real fairy tale.

This miraculous state of affairs lasted for several years and might have gone on some time longer. But, beyond my euphoria, beyond the warm light-hearted atmosphere they generated between them, the sinister threat in the background was always waiting. Disaster loomed over them like a circle of icy mountains, implacably drawing nearer: they'd developed a special attitude in self-defence. Because crashes and constant danger made each man die many times, they spoke of death as an ordinary event, for which the carelessness or recklessness of the individual was wholly responsible. Nobody ever said 'Poor old Z's had it' but 'Z asked for it, the crazy bastard, never more than one jump ahead of the mortuary.' Their jargon had a brutal sound to outsiders. But, by speaking derisively of the victim, they deprived death of terror, made it seem something he could easily have avoided.

Without conscious reflection, I took it for granted that, when the time came, I would die on the track like my friends, and this very nearly happened. The car crashed and turned four somersaults before it burst into flames, and the driver and the other passengers were killed instantly. I had the extreme bad luck to be dragged out of the blazing wreckage only three-quarters dead. Apparently my case was a challenge to the doctors of several hospitals, who, for the next two years, worked with obstinate persistence to save my life, while I persistently tried to discard it. I used to look in their cold, clinical eyes with loathing and helpless rage. They got their way in the end and discharged me. I was pushed out again into the hateful world, alone, hardly able to walk and disfigured by burns.

The drivers loyally kept in touch, wrote and sent presents to the hospitals, came to see me whenever they could. It was entirely my own fault that, as the months dragged on, the letters became fewer, the visits less and less frequent, until they finally ceased. I didn't want them to be sorry for me or to feel any obligation. I was sure my scarred face must repel them, so I deliberately drove them away.

I couldn't possibly go back to them: I had no heart, no vitality, for the life I'd so much enjoyed. I was no longer the gay, adventurous girl they had liked. All the same, if one of them had really exerted himself to persuade me, I might . . . That nobody made this special effort, or showed a desire for further intimacy, confirmed my conviction that I had become repulsive. Although there was a possible alternative explanation. At the time of the crash, I had been in love with the man who was driving and hadn't yet reached the stage of singling out his successor. So, as I was the one who always took the initiative, none of them had any cause to feel closer to me than the rest. Perhaps if I had indicated a preference . . . But I was paralysed by the guilt of my survival, as certain they all resented my being alive as if I'd caused their comrade's death.

What can I do now? What am I to become? How can I live in this world I'm condemned to but can't endure? They couldn't stand it either, so they made a world of their own. Well, they have each other's company, and they are heroes, whereas I'm quite alone and have none of the qualities essential to heroism – the spirit, the toughness, the dedication. I'm back where I was as a child: solitary, helpless, unwanted, frightened.

It's so lonely, so terribly lonely. I hate being always alone. I so badly need someone to talk to, someone to love. Nobody looks at me now, and I don't want them to; I don't want to be seen. I can't bear to look at myself in the glass. I keep away from people as much as I can. I know everyone is repelled and embarrassed by all these scars.

There is no kindness left. The world is a cruel place full of men I shall never know, whose indifference terrifies me. If once in a way I catch someone's eye, his glance is as cold as ice, eyes look past eyes like searchlights crossing, with no more humanity or communication. In freezing despair, I walk down the street, trying to attract to myself a suggestion of warmth by showing in my expression . . . something . . . or something . . . And everybody walks past me, refusing to see or to lift a finger. No one cares, no one will help me. An abstract impenetrable indifference in a stranger's eye is all I ever see.

The world belongs to heartless people and to machines which can't give. Only the others, the heroes, know how to give. Out of their great generosity they gave me the truth, paid me the compliment of not lying to me. Not one of them ever told me life was worth living. They are the only people I've ever loved. I think only of them and of how they are lost to me. How never again shall I sit beside someone who loves me while the world races past. Never again cross the tropic of Capricorn, or, under the Arctic stars, in the blackness of firs and spruce, see the black glitter of ice in starlight in the cold snow countries.

The world in which I was really alive consisted of hotel bedrooms and one man in a car. But that world was enormous and splendid, containing cities and continents, forests and seas and mountains, plants and animals, the Pole Star and the Southern Cross. The heroes who showed me how to live also showed me everything, everywhere in the world.

My present world is reduced to their remembered faces, which have gone for ever, which get further and further away. I don't feel alive any more. I see nothing at all of the outside world. There are no more oceans or mountains for me.

I don't look up now. I always try not to look at the stars. I can't bear to see them, because the stars remind me of loving and of being loved.

JULIA AND THE BAZOOKA

JULIA IS A LITTLE girl with long straight hair and big eyes. Julia loved flowers. In the cornfield she has picked an enormous untidy bunch of red poppies which she is holding up so that most of her face is hidden except the eyes. Her eyes look sad because she has just been told to throw the poppies away, not to bring them inside to make a mess dropping their petals all over the house. Some of them have shed their petals already; the front of her dress is quite red. Julia is also a quiet schoolgirl who does not make many friends. Then she is a tall student standing with other students who have passed their final examinations, whose faces are gay and excited, eager to start life in the world. Only Julia's eyes are sad. Although she smiles with the others, she does not share their enthusiasm for living. She feels cut off from people. She is afraid of the world.

Julia is also a young bride in a white dress, holding a sheaf of roses in one hand and in the other a very small flat white satin bag containing a lace-edged handkerchief scented with Arpège and a plastic syringe. Now Julia's eyes are not at all sad. She has one foot on the step of a car, its door held open by a young man with kinky brown hair and a rose in his buttonhole. She is laughing because of something he's said or because he has just squeezed her arm or because she no longer feels frightened or cut off now that she has the syringe. A group of indistinct people in the background look on approvingly as if they are glad to transfer responsibility for Julia to the young man. Julia who loves flowers waves to them with her roses as she drives off with him.

Julia is also dead without any flowers. The doctor sighs when he looks at her lying there. No one else comes to look except the official people. The ashes of the tall girl Julia barely fill the silver cup she won in the tennis tournament. To improve her game the tennis professional gives her the syringe. He is a joking kind of man and calls the syringe a bazooka. Julia calls it that, too. The name sounds funny, it makes her laugh. Of course, she knows all the sensational stories about drug addiction, but the word bazooka makes nonsense of them, makes the whole drug business seem not serious. Without the bazooka she might not have won the cup, which as a container will at last serve a useful purpose. It is Julia's serve that wins the decisive game. Holding two tennis balls in her left hand, she throws one high in the air while her right hand flies up over her head, brings the racket down, wham, and sends the ball skimming over the opposite court hardly bouncing at all, a service almost impossible to return. Holding two balls in her hand Julia also lies in bed beside the young man with kinky hair. Julia is also lying in wreckage under an army blanket, and eventually Julia's ashes go into the silver cup.

The undertaker or somebody closes the lid and locks the cup in a pigeon-hole among thousands of identical pigeon-holes in a wall at the top of a cliff overlooking the sea. The winter sea is the colour of pumice, the sky cold as grey ice, the icy wind charges straight at the wall making it tremble so that the silver cup in its pigeon-hole shivers and tinkles faintly. The wind is trying to tear to pieces a few frost-bitten flowers which have not been left for Julia at the foot of the wall. Julia is also driving with her bridegroom in the high mountains through fields of flowers. They stop the car and pick armfuls of daffodils and narcissi. There are no flowers for Julia in the pigeon-hole and no bridegroom either.

'This is her syringe, her bazooka she always called it,' the doctor says with a small sad smile. 'It must be twenty years old at least. Look how the measures have been worn away by continuous use.' The battered old plastic syringe is unbreakable, unlike the glass syringes which used to be kept in boiled water in metal boxes and reasonably sterile. This discoloured old syringe has always been left lying about somewhere, accumulating germs and the assorted dirt of wars and cities. All the same, it has not done Julia any great harm. An occasional infection easily cured with penicillin, nothing serious. 'Such dangers are grossly exaggerated.'

Julia and her bazooka travel all over the world. She wants to see everything, every country. The young man with kinky hair is not there, but she is in a car and somebody sits beside her. Julia is a good driver. She drives anything, racing cars, heavy lorries. Her long hair streams out from under the crash helmet as she drives for the racing teams. Today she is lapping only a fraction of a second behind the number-one driver when a red-hot bit of his clutch flies off and punctures her nearside tyre, and the car somersaults twice and tears through a wall. Julia steps out of the wreck uninjured and walks away holding her handbag with the syringe inside it. She is laughing. Julia always laughs at danger. Nothing can frighten her while she has the syringe. She has almost forgotten the time when she was afraid. Sometimes she thinks of the kinky-haired man and wonders what he is doing. Then she laughs. There are always plenty of people to bring her flowers and make her feel gay. She hardly remembers how sad and lonely she used to feel before she had the syringe.

Julia likes the doctor as soon as she meets him. He is understanding and kind like the father she has imagined but never known. He does not want to take her syringe away. He says, 'You've used it for years already, and you're none the worse. In fact, you'd be far worse off without it.' He trusts Julia, he knows she is not irresponsible; she does not increase the dosage too much or experiment with new drugs. It is ridiculous to say all drug addicts are alike, all liars, all vicious, all psychopaths or delinquents just out for kicks. He is sympathetic towards Julia whose personality has been damaged by no love in childhood so that she can't make contact with people or feel at home in the world. In his opinion she is quite right to use the syringe; it is as essential to her as insulin to a diabetic. Without it she could not lead a normal existence, her life would be a shambles, but with its support she is conscientious and energetic, intelligent, friendly. She is most unlike the popular notion of a drug addict. Nobody could call her vicious.

Julia who loves flowers has made a garden on a flat roof in the city; all around her are pots of scarlet geraniums. Throughout the summer she has watered them every day because the pots dry out so fast up here in the sun and wind. Now summer is over, there is frost in the air. The leaves of the plants have turned yellow. Although the flowers have survived up to now the next frost will finish them off. It is wartime, the time of the flying bombs. They come over all the time; there seems to be nothing to stop them. Julia is used to them, she ignores them, she does not look. To save the flowers from the frost she picks them all quickly and takes them indoors. Then it is winter, and Julia is on the roof planting bulbs to flower in the spring. The flying bombs are still coming over, quite low, just above roofs and chimneys; their chugging noise fills the sky. One after another, they keep coming over, making their monotonous mechanical noise. When the engine cuts out there is a sudden startling silence, suspense, everything suddenly goes unnaturally still. Julia does not look up when the silence comes, but all at once it seems very cold on the roof, and she plants the last bulb in a hurry.

The doctor has gone to consult a top psychiatrist about one of his patients. The psychiatrist is immensely dignified, extremely well dressed; his voice matches his outer aspect. When the bomb silence starts, his clear grave voice says solemnly, 'I advise you to take cover under that table beside you', as he himself glides with the utmost dignity under his impressive desk. Julia leaves the roof and steps on to the staircase, which is not there. The stairs have crumbled, the whole house is crumbling, collapsing, the world bursts and burns, while she falls through the dark. The ARP men dig Julia out of the rubble. Red geraniums are spilling down the front of her dress; she has forgotten the time between and is forgetting more and more every moment. Someone spreads a grey blanket over her; she lies underneath it in her red-stained dress, her bag, with the bazooka inside, safely hooked over one arm. How cold it is in the exploding world. The Northern Lights burst out in frigid brilliance across the sky. The ice roars and thunders like gunfire. The cold is glacial, a glass dome of cold covers the globe. Icebergs tower high as mountains, furious blizzards swoop at each other like white wild beasts. All things are turning to ice in the mortal cold, and the cold has a face which sparkles with frost. It seems to be a face Julia knows, although she has forgotten whose face it is.

The undertaker hurriedly shuts himself inside his car, out of the cruel wind. The parson hurries towards his house, hatless, thin grey hair blowing about wildly. The wind snatches a tattered wreath of frost-blackened flowers and rolls it over the grass, past the under-taker and the parson, who both pretend not to see. They are not going to stay out in the cold any longer; it is not their job to look after the flowers. They do not know that Julia loves flowers, and they do not care. The wreath was not put there for her anyhow.

Julia is rushing after the nameless face, running as fast as if she was playing tennis. But when she comes near she does not, after all, recognize that glittering death-mask. It has gone now; there's nothing but Arctic glitter; she is a bride again beside the young man with brown hair. The lights are blazing, but she shivers a little in her thin dress because the church is so cold. The dazzling brilliance of the aurora borealis has burned right through the roof with its frigid fire. Snow slants down between the rafters, there is ice on the altar, snowdrifts in the aisles, the holy water and the communion wine have been frozen solid. Snow is Julia's bridal white, icicles are her jewels. The diamond-sparkling coronet on her head confuses her thoughts. Where has everyone gone? The bridegroom is dead or in bed with some girl or other, and she herself lies under a dirty blanket with red on her dress.

'Won't somebody help me?' she calls. 'I can't move.' But no one takes any notice. She is not cold any longer. Suddenly now she is burning, a fever is burning her up. Her face is on fire, her dry mouth seems to be full of ashes. She sees the kind doctor coming and tries to call him but can only whisper, 'Please help me . . .' so faintly that he does not hear. Sighing, he takes off his hat, gazing down at his name printed inside in small gold letters under the leather band. The kinky-haired young man is not in bed with anyone. He is wounded in a sea battle. He falls on the warship's deck. An officer tries to grab him, but it's too late; over and over he rolls down the steeply sloping deck to the black bottomless water. The officer looks over the side, holding a lifebelt, but does not throw it down to the injured man; instead, he puts it on himself and runs to a boat which is being lowered. The doctor comes home from the house of the famous psychiatrist. His head is bent, his eyes lowered. He walks slowly because he feels tired and sad. He does not look up, so he never sees Julia waving to him with a bunch of geraniums from the window.

The pigeon-hole wall stands deserted in the cold dusk. The under-taker has driven home. His feet are so cold he can't feel them; these winter funerals are the very devil. He slams the car door, goes inside stamping his feet and shouts to his wife to bring, double quick, a good strong hot rum with plenty of lemon and sugar in case he has caught a chill. The wife, who was just going out to a bingo session, grumbles at being delayed and bangs about in the kitchen. At the vicarage the parson is eating a crumpet for tea, his chair pulled so close to the fire that he is practically in the grate.

It has got quite dark outside; the wall has turned black. As the wind shakes it, the faintest of tinkles comes from the pigeon-hole where all that is left of Julia has been left. Surely there were some red flowers somewhere, Julia would be thinking, if she could still think. Then she would think something amusing, she would remember the bazooka and start to laugh. But nothing is left of Julia really; she is not there. The only occupant of the pigeon-hole is the silver cup, which can't think or laugh or remember. There is no more Julia anywhere. Where she was there is only nothing.

FIVE MORE DAYS TO COUNTDOWN

THE SITUATION IS RATHER dodgy. We may get away with it. But I wish I could persuade Esmerelda to leave now, in case things get worse. Does she, or does she not, really mean to come away with me finally to some lost Antipodean island? It's hard to tell.

She's a strange woman. People are perplexed by her stark Nordic strangeness and Lorelei hair and by her eyes which have the remote blue glitter of the Skagerrak. It's not how they expect the founder and principal of an important college to look. I point out to them, whenever a suitable opening occurs, that a brilliant, unorthodox superwoman, the inventor of a revolutionary system of education, isn't likely to conform to ordinary standards in her appearance or anything else.

Meanwhile, the students have got out of hand. Impossible to keep them inside our walls. They're all over the town, the streets are full of them. Shoulder to shoulder, they march about, singing their rude fraternity songs and carrying banners with subversive slogans. No one's quite sure what they want or why they are demonstrating. Yesterday they closed ranks and barricaded the marketplace and the main street for hours. The townspeople are indignant. They can't do their shopping, and Christmas is only five days ahead. A deputation of shopkeepers has just been to the college demanding immediate action. Esmerelda was experimenting with a new snow-wheat hairpiece, so I got rid of them, with considerable difficulty. They didn't want to go without seeing her and left reluctantly, muttering, shaking their fists at me, threatening to ask for government protection unless we get the students under control at once. If they do that, we're sunk.

'It will be fatal if they ask for protection,' I told Esmerelda. 'The authorities will take over, and we'll be kicked out.'

'They'd never dare get rid of *me*.' Her eyes flashed, she stuck out her chin, asserting herself as a superwoman. Asserting herself some more, she went on, 'Don't forget I invented this revolutionary educational system.'

'Which they now see breaking down. You'd much better come away with me while the going's good.'

A dedicated idealist if ever there was one, she insisted that it was her duty to stay. 'And yours, too. Especially as things are.' She looked at me coldly out of her northern eyes, which are sometimes so blue they are almost purple.

She certainly is a strange woman. In a century which has exalted war to unprecedented heights, regarding it as the finest flower of human endeavour and scientific progress, subordinating everything else in life to it as a matter of course, she sees the all-powerful giant mushroom shape menacing us as a mere bogey to be eliminated simply by depriving children of war-like toys.

'Teach the kids of all nations together,' she says. 'Instead of telling them they're Aryans, Asians, Africans or whatever, call them all humans, and bring them all up the same way. Then they'll take their different-coloured skins for granted. There'll be no more colour problem and no more war.' The superb simplicity of the concept is staggering. At first, I was absolutely carried away by her extraordinary vision, by her enthusiasm and by the enormous grants and awards she extracted from pacifist organizations. Now I sometimes wonder if she's not incredibly naïve; except that such naïvety passes belief. The success of her theory depends on segregating the students; but it's proved impossible to isolate them completely from the world outside. Outsiders, of course, are responsible for the present trouble: war is their god and their religion, and they've infected our lot with their pernicious beliefs.

The position is becoming more dangerous. The students are now out in force, and we can do nothing with them. Only the children in the junior section still keep to their usual routine. 'Those blessed innocents remain uncontaminated,' said Esmerelda. 'They won't let me down.' I hoped she was right, thought it wiser to say no more. She's crazy about the juniors, teaches them herself. In one lesson she teaches them about the galaxies, Kublai Khan and dimensional limitations. Those kids' heads must be whizzing round. Who can guess what's going on inside them?

Student riots have reduced the town to a state of chaos. 'Public indignation is rising,' I told her. 'Things look pretty grim.' 'Well, why don't you do something about it?' she snapped back at me. 'Don't just stand there . . .' It wasn't like her; she doesn't snap as a rule. I saw that she was wearing a new pair of Chapal tiger-patterned, kid knee-high boots and guessed they were hurting her – she will buy them a size too small. I organized the staff into patrols, issued armbands and sent them out to do what they could to restore order. Regrettably, some of them failed to return and were said to have joined the rebels.

Disregarding a sensational rumour that student orgies were taking place with drink, psychedelic drugs and naked girls coated in aspic, I drove around, searching for the leaders. I was waiting for the traffic lights to change colour when some heavy metal thing shattered the window beside me and flashed past my head. A six-foot lance neatly transfixed the width of the car. My face was cut, with blood getting into my eyes. I only just caught sight of a running figure disappearing among the traffic. I started off in pursuit but was held up again. When I saw another man with a lance waiting at the next corner, I whipped around, raced back to college and telephoned the police.

It is reported that communists have approached the students who, instead of repulsing them, are letting themselves be trained and organized into smooth-functioning units, equipped with Lugers, an enlarged vocabulary, aerosols and slinky stretch-pants in glittering fabric. I passed a crowd of our girls clustered together, suspected them of concealing communists in their midst. But the glitter was too bright, I was dazzled and saw nothing clearly: in the end I was forced to avert my eyes. In the hope of luring them back to normal, I set out supplies of heroin and cocaine in the classrooms, off-duty silk shirts and luxuriant eyelashes; decorated the walls with make-up artists of top sex appeal. The results, frankly, were disappointing.

Esmerelda opened the door of my room, looking every inch a superwoman in patent cavalier shoes with detachable buckles of red lizard and silver and holding a pretty but useless wicker fly-swatter in one hand. 'What's happened to your face?' I asked her. She spoke of an emblem worn by taxi drivers in Jamiltepec to ward off the evil eye. 'How is the situation?' she inquired. In my straightforward, manly way, I replied, 'Bad. The government places a sinister interpretation on the student–communist axis. It would be wise to leave while the way is open.' Her cold eyes withered me, she hit the side of my head twice with the fly-swatter, breaking it, and then left the room. Frankly, I was puzzled by her reactions.

I decided to prepare for the worst. In the dead of night, without telling anyone, I secreted my helicopter among dense bushes in the shrubbery at the back of the main building. There it will remain, from now on, ready for us, in case we have to make a quick getaway. Nobody ever goes there at this time of year; it's perfectly safe, hidden behind the pendulous branches of thick evergreens.

Shouts, screams, a mounting crescendo of threatening noise from the town sent me hurrying across the grounds. Ya-hoo-hee! Ya-hoo-hee! Closer shrieks came from a crawly horror in a red catsuit with insignia in four colours. Scores of pygmies closed in; each had on a steel helmet decorated with this splendid four-colour-job mushroom; each pointed a pistol at me.

'Stick your hands up!' howled a khaki character (communist?) on the all-kill wavelength, who appeared to be in command. 'And keep them up there – my gun has real bullets in it!' The pygmy ambush took me by surprise, preoccupied as I was with events in the town, but it was easily dealt with. I asked what they wanted, promised careful consideration of reasonable demands, which were to be made in writing.

A sack of mail, directed to Santa, was delivered later. Sifting through the contents, through the requests for definitive trendy kaftans, *avant-garde* night caps, exciting fab fun-fur hoods, switched-on gear of all kinds, I found the more basic items. Junior practical fighting techniques. Guerrilla warfare for the under-sixteens, including training in hand-to-hand combat. Do-it-yourself weapons for schools: simple construction of mortars, flamethrowers, ballistic missiles. How to construct an ambush, a booby trap. Useful tips on terrorism, napalm, nuclear devices, with sections on robbery with violence, blackmail, piracy on the high seas, arson, karate.

I saw Esmerelda walking across the snowy lawn beside the gymnasium and went out to meet her. On one wall of the gym an immature hand had daubed in white paint: Give us Guns not Games at Yule or you'll go Ezzie. It was blasphemy. I wondered how they had dared . . . 'Bad news.' I prepared her gravely. 'The juniors are defecting, ganging up with the others against us.' I couldn't keep it from her, she had to know. 'I don't believe it.' Her eyes were arctic. I pointed silently to the painted message. 'Oh, no . . .' she moaned, stricken. I put my hand on her arm, looked at her with my kind, understanding expression. 'You see? It's hopeless. Why don't you face the facts? Your dream is over. Come with me while we're still free to find peace and security.'

Ya-hoo-hee! Ya-hoo-hee! Ya-hoo-hee! A sudden chorus of blood-curdling yells split the air. I gripped her hand, pulled her along with me towards the main portico at the end of the lawn. 'Come on – we must run for it!' Hordes of stampeding pygmies pursued us with terrifying war cries. I heard twanging bows, cried, 'Faster, faster!' as their arrows showered around us. She gasped, 'I can't . . . my shoes . . .' 'Take them off. Those arrows are tipped in curare.' On we flew, she in her stockinged feet. There wasn't a moment to lose, their feet pounded behind us, their Indian clubs thundered on the grass. Not a moment too soon, we reached the shelter of the portico. I dragged her inside the building and locked the door. It had been a near thing.

I said, 'A near thing.' She was smiling her strange smile. She had her shoes in her hand, now she put them on, while I regarded her with admiration. In her study, I read out some of the juniors' war-like demands. She interrupted me, snatched the paper, tore it up, threw the fragments away. 'They've disappointed me. I thought better of them.' I made an attempt to explain. 'Kids need these things nowadays. You can't put the clock back –' Not a moment too soon, I swung her away from the window. Seven bullets pierced it, leaving seven round holes in the glass in the shape of the Plough. Outside, pygmy figures in khaki and battle helmets danced up and down, chanting, 'The youngest generation demands the right to participate in the war against criminal aggression.' Pointing their guns again, they rasped, 'Kill! Kill! Kill!' We stole away through the deepening shadows over the broken glass.

Rioting students have brought the life of the town to a standstill. Our secret informant reports that the mayor has sent an urgent request for military aid, government forces are coming, an attack can be expected on Christmas Day. On Esmerelda's order I sent radio messages to the rebels. 'The government will crush you and the communists together. You don't stand an earthly chance, so surrender to us.' I told her that they refused to listen. She said, 'Then I shall speak to them myself. Everything must be back to normal when these government people arrive.' She *is* a strange woman. She was smiling again. 'Just watch their faces when they find us carrying on as usual. I'll show that fool of a mayor what's really what and who is really on top.' I said, 'It'll take some arm-twisting to get the students back here.' She drew herself up to her full height. 'Of course, they'll respond to my magic. I've mesmerized them for years.' One has to admire such confidence. All the same, I was nervous. Suppose they'd had enough of her magic? 'You can't trust them,' I tried to dissuade her. 'They are desperate and will stop at nothing. The whole town is seething with hate and violence. For the love of God, Esmerelda, belt up. You need rest, my love. Come with me to some unexplored island or far-off plateau in the mountains, far from drug-crazed teenagers and delinquent subteens.' Her glance was straight from the polar regions. 'They will be here tonight,' she said.

Later, announcing triumphantly that the magic had worked, she ordered a buffet supper to be laid out in the dining hall. 'They'll never be able to resist the food, and once they start eating they'll be easy to handle.'

Ten minutes before the time set for the meeting, the staff assembled in that large, lofty apartment with black-and-red Aztec designs and ambiguous paintings on the walls. I was gloomy. I feared a trap. Esmerelda sat in the centre with some of the older professors; the rest of us remained standing. Would the students come? I surveyed faces; everybody was getting dubious, to say the least. Only Esmerelda looked perfectly calm, relaxed, self-assured, insulated by a shock of sheer electricity, clear-cut by Christian Dior, lean leggy acid-blue tights sparkled with golden paillettes, translucent gold shoes under her chair. She had just slipped the shoes off to demonstrate to us how thoroughly she was at ease. There are moments when I adore that woman. The physics professor beside her had also kicked off his shoes; but I noticed his toes were twitching – a sure sign of nerves.

The clock struck. Zero hour. Still no students. Thought waves pulsated between the walls, sound waves were audible. Figures appeared. But who were they? Students? Communists? Or the others? They looked like our students, dressed in these boring tight jeans and sweatshirts covered with stupid cars and top-pop titles. But how could one know that they hadn't just assumed student identity?

Esmerelda (if she *was* Esmerelda) started talking to them. The girls' glittery legs moved like running water, and I wondered what acts of violence would be perpetrated when things got going. The curtains had not been drawn, the big windows divided the walls into a series of black arcades. I saw a mysterious movement in the dark and stepped out to investigate, suspecting treachery of some kind. Sure enough, hostile figures were everywhere; we were surrounded by strategically placed mortars trained on the main building. Rushing back, I re-entered the dining hall just as people were starting to help themselves to the food. 'Break it up! The party's over!' I cried. 'Those fish fingers are poisoned.' All over the room, forks clattered on plates, excited, angry or frightened voices shouted questions which I ignored. Grabbing Esmerelda's arm, I muttered into her ear, 'Come quickly! We've been tricked. We're encircled by irregular troops.' She held back, groping about on the floor for her shoes. 'Come on! We must fly,' I insisted, seeing her suspended above the rooftops on wide superwoman wings. With more than my usual force and determination (was it somebody else's?) I propelled her through an inconspicuous door at the back, directly opposite the concealed helicopter. Hand in hand we sprinted across the snow, as a howling mob burst out of the building we'd left and came tearing after us. In the nick of time, I heaved her into the machine, climbed up myself. Shots exploded, everybody was yelling, flares lit distorted, unrecognizable faces, searchlights pursued us into the black unknown.

Up, up we soared, far above questionable students, leaving the noisy commotion far behind us. The whirlybird whirled us away on our search for peace. I looked at my winged superwoman, saw no Skagerrak glint in her eyes, which were ringed by romantic lashes and painted black all around.

What a strange woman she is. Her strangeness is a sort of charisma, a special divine gift. She's been invited to the palace to lunch with the Queen. Her picture is on the front cover of *Vogue*. And then she's so talented and intelligent. (But is she Esmerelda?)

In my gold and purple, with my rings and robes, I feel worthy to be her companion. (But who the hell am I supposed to be?) The situation this Yuletide is somewhat obscure. I assume, however, that we are all involved in the same old concerns. (The war in Asia. This love thing.) Esmerelda and I are swinging high over the world, conveyed through a sky full of snow by eight polar bears, whose bells jingle. Gosh, I never expected a happy ending.

STARTING A CAREER

THIS YOUNG FELLOW, STRANGE young fellow I'd never seen in my life, walked into my room without knocking. He was wearing a shiny white helmet, was otherwise all black leather and looked a tough sort of weapon-trained man. Disliking his invasion of my living space, I demanded, 'Who the hell are you? What's the gatecrashing idea?'

Without a word, he thrust a long envelope at me. I broke the enormous official seal, found inside a summons to attend Lord Legion's court the next day. This was incredible, crazy, as I'd just started to work for the President's party, which was the opposition. Everyone knew the President hated Lord Legion and Lord Legion hated the President. I couldn't go near Legion's court without losing my job. 'It's not for me. It must be a mistake,' I said. 'Or if it's some sort of joke I don't think it's funny.' I threw the document at him; he caught it neatly and flicked it back. 'It's for you, all right. Lord Legion doesn't make mistakes.' He'd disappeared before I could speak again.

I examined the paper more closely, decided it must be genuine. No joker would have gone to the trouble of reproducing that ancient parchment and wording, even if it had been possible. Lord Legion's court was a survival from the remote past, an anachronism, a mystery. Legion himself was a mystery man of whom nothing was known. It was a mystery what he could want with me. The longer I thought about it, the more mystified I became. Could I have offended him in some way? My conscience was clear. But it was always possible I had infringed some obsolete regulation I'd never heard of. There must be any number of idiotical laws still unrepealed which could be conveniently invoked against anybody he wished to incriminate. But why should he want to incriminate me? I was too insignificant. In fact, I was amazed that he'd even heard of me or knew anything about me. Of course, there were said to be secret devices . . .

Nobody knew the court's exact function; there were only rumours. People said its powers equalled those of the President, its ancient legislature representing reactionary forces as opposed to his forward-looking, up-to-date policies. I'd never known anyone who'd had deal-ings with it and had always thought of it as a relic of the Middle Ages, allowed to survive because it attracted tourists. To find it suddenly invading my personal life was disturbing to say the least. My impulse was to ignore the summons. But if I did that a sergeant-at-arms or someone would probably come and arrest me, which wouldn't do my reputation much good. Whatever I did I would be in trouble. It looked as if my career would be over almost before it began. Looking at the thing again, I read: 'Lord Legion's court is in session 365 days a year, sits 24 hours a day and has complete jurisdiction over all civil, military and penal affairs.' Well, that seemed to be that. Yes, I was in trouble, all right. Bad trouble.

It was midwinter. When I set out late the next afternoon it was snowing hard. The snow at least was on my side, keeping people indoors; there was nobody in the streets to watch where I was going. Snow was piling up everywhere, making things look strange. In the fading light, the tremendous mass of the courthouse, sombre, secretive, seemed to crouch like some fabulous monster, evoking childish nocturnal fears I had quite forgotten. Suppressing them by an effort of will, I banged my fist on the huge medieval gateway, a section of which moved to admit me. Inside, two machine-gun nests guarded the entrance, invisible from the road.

Soldiers checked my credentials, took me across a courtyard, past another guard post and into the main buildings, where I was left with a man speaking into a telephone. Passing the instrument to me, he told me to state my business. I was determined not to appear nervous and held my head high, my chin up, while I said boldly into the mouthpiece, 'My business is with Lord Legion.' Immediately a suave voice replied. 'Legion speaking.' I was staggered. I almost dropped the receiver. Fancy him answering the phone himself, just like anyone else! I would be interviewed at once, he informed me, when I gave my name.

Promptly, a whole procession of officers-at-arms, heralds, etc. came marching along a corridor as wide as the Irrawaddy to escort me to him, with all their antique mumbo jumbo of drums, torches and tasselled trumpets. I was blindfolded, put through an odd kind of drill. Sit. Stand. Kneel. About turn. Three steps forward. Back – presumably to confuse my sense of direction, before, eyes still bandaged, I was guided along passages, through doorways guarded by sentries, up a short staircase and finally left alone to wait. Blinking in the sudden blaze of electric light, I surveyed a large room, grandly furnished with scrolled and gilded pieces of the Second Empire period, the panelled walls hung with portraits of imposing figures in archaic dress. Perhaps one of them was Lord Legion. I was curious to know what he looked like. No photographs of him were ever published; he never appeared on television. Several quite different descriptions of him were in circulation. He was said to be: a sinister dwarf, always dressed entirely in black; a very tall thin man with a blond beard; a fierce, bad-tempered man like a charging bull. None of these proved to be accurate.

Magnificently dressed officers entered, many-coloured ribbons across their chests, gold cords looped over their shoulders, forming a bodyguard around a central figure so caked in white that he looked like a snowman. 'Lord Legion!' someone announced loudly. I clicked my heels, saluted, stood to attention, wondering why he'd gone out after speaking to me on the phone. Or perhaps the voice I'd heard hadn't been his at all.

He faced me in dead silence, stared at me fixedly, then, with a startlingly loud, sharp noise, clapped his gloved hands together, showering snow all over a nearby sofa. As an opening gesture it was effective, seemed to have been rehearsed. I regarded him doubtfully, as, assisted by a dark, handsome young man in a white uniform, he began unwrapping himself, practically in slow motion, removing each garment with deliberation before handing it to his aide. All the time he was pulling off his gloves, shaking his fur hat and divesting himself of his splendid seal-lined overcoat, he kept his eyes on me as if I was a mirror in which he was watching his own reflection. It was embarrassing. I felt more than uncomfortable – distinctly uneasy.

He was a strange-looking man, not at all like the President or any of the important people I'd met. Without his overcoat, he made an impression of cold remoteness, his dark civilian suit contrasting strangely with the gorgeous clothes and colours worn by his entourage He had thick grey hair, a large carved face with lines running up and down it and an expression I couldn't decipher. He went on staring at me out of eyes set deep like recessed spotlights under the ridge of brows. I wished he would speak, say what he wanted with me. The silent stare was becoming rather unnerving.

At length he sat down in an armchair covered in red velvet, and, still in silence, indicated that I was to take the chair opposite. I felt more nervous than ever, confronted so closely by that sculptured face. The silence went on and on; I was thinking I wouldn't be able to stand it much longer, when he suddenly laughed.

'Well, you can keep your mouth shut, at any rate.' I was not at all sure that this was meant to be complimentary but hoped for the best since he now poured two small glasses of brandy from a decanter which stood on a gilded table and pushed one towards me, saying, 'Let's drink to our better acquaintance.' Directly afterwards, he leaned forward and added in a low tone no one else could have heard, 'And may the association prove profitable to us both.'

Wondering what on earth that could mean, I regarded him surreptitiously over my glass as I drank his health but learned nothing from his impassive countenance.

'I need not keep you gentlemen any longer,' he told the officers, who were still standing around in a stiff circle. As they filed out, he detained the young man I'd already noticed, catching hold of his sleeve and pulling him down to whisper into his ear. Astonished by the familiarity of this action, so out of keeping with his formal, remote appearance, I felt bewildered, out of my depth altogether. What was going on? Why was I here? The whole situation was quite beyond me. I wanted to interrupt the whispering by demanding to be told why I'd been summoned. Then, all at once, I saw the good-looking fellow on his way to the door, where he glanced around, caught my eye and winked deliberately, thus completing my total confusion.

However, Lord Legion's next words sounded encouraging. 'I hear the President finds you most useful.' It seemed safe to say, 'All I want is to be of service to him.' But this merely elicited the dry, disapproving retort, 'A limited and emotional point of view.' I decided that I knew nothing. He was staring at me again. 'Well, haven't you got anything to tell me?' The question was put sharply and still more disapprovingly. I got the impression some specific reply was expected but had no idea what it was. Frowning and drumming his fingers on the table, he said in an ominous tone, 'I'm beginning to think we're just wasting time.' I knew nothing about anything. The mixture of impatience, anger and disappointment in his voice made me stammer something apologetic about my own youth and inexperience, reminding him that I'd only lately left college.

Gazing fixedly at me, he remarked, 'The professors report that you learn very quickly and have an exceptionally good memory. It seems a pity to restrict your talents to one limited sphere.' A wild notion entered my head. I suppressed it as too fantastic to contemplate. Although it seemed less crazy when he continued, 'Has it never occurred to you that talent should be pooled for the common good?' Was it possible . . . ? Surely it couldn't be . . . and yet . . . With growing excitement I heard, 'I believe all information should be made available for the maximum benefit of the state.' There was a slight pause, then, 'You have access to certain information and are in a position to pass it on. Useful items, of course, have their market value.'

So my idea *had* been right, incredible as it seemed. At last the reason why I'd been sent for was clear – at last I had grasped it. Astounding vistas began to open before *me*. But, next moment, I was uncertain again. This couldn't be happening to me; it was too wildly improbable. I must be dreaming. I was afraid to speak in case I'd been mistaken; until it suddenly struck me that my silence might be misconstrued. Hurriedly, I swallowed a mouthful of brandy, kept my fingers crossed and said cautiously, 'Thank you for speaking plainly. Of course, I understand now.'

'And what do you say? Are you prepared to cooperate with me?' His amused sidelong look was undoubtedly real. This was no dream – it was actually happening. What amazing luck! What a marvellous chance to increase my income! Suddenly I could hardly control my excitement. It was a great effort to say calmly, 'Certainly. Provided the market value makes it worth my while.' I couldn't think why I had been so stupid as not to realize that my intelligence had a value over and above my salary. It was all I could do to remain outwardly cool and collected while he replied, surprising me with a grin, 'As long as you supply the goods you can count on a generous remuneration.' At the same time he unlocked a hidden drawer in the gilded table, extracted a fat envelope and handed it to me. 'This advance should remove your doubts.'

I thanked him. We both stood up. My head was spinning, my heart beating faster than usual. I knew I had reached an important crossroads in my existence. How differently the interview had turned out from what I had feared. Instead of ruining my career, it had opened the way to one far more thrilling and lucrative.

'The captain will be your contact in future,' Lord Legion was saying. The handsome young man had reappeared as promptly as if he'd been waiting outside the door. 'Do as he tells you, and you'll be making a significant contribution to the welfare of the country.'

But it was my own welfare I was thinking about as, pushing the envelope into my pocket, I saluted and left the room beside the man in the white uniform. He was obviously alert and high-spirited; I thought we should get on well. But I was glad he only came with me as far as the outer gate, which we reached by a much shorter route than the one I had come by. I needed to be alone now, to reflect on all that had taken place, to organize my whirling thoughts and adjust myself to my new role and the wonderful potentialities ahead.

In the darkness, big white flakes were still falling thickly out of the unseen sky. It seemed right and appropriate that snow had hidden the familiar town, revealing another, mysterious, muffled, as different from the place I had always known as my present expanding ideas differed from the small preoccupations of boyhood and adolescence. I hardly recognized my surroundings but followed the empty, snow-bound streets by instinct, oblivious of the cold; delirious visions of future exploits were keeping me warm.

Touching the envelope in my pocket, I thought of tremendous balances accumulating, safe and secret, in various banks around the world, ready to confer on me the supreme power only money can give. Why shouldn't I work for the secret services of two, three, four, five, six – any number of countries? I felt drunk, exhilarated, carried away, imagining meetings with foreign intelligence chiefs in secret cells under the Alps or the Andes, on satellites in space or bathyspheres on the ocean floor, with tough, beautiful girls who seduced men with their burning languorous eyes or vaporized them with electronic blasters.

Already I saw myself becoming a legend, an insoluble mystery. No one, knowing me as an inconspicuous cog in the Presidential machine, my personality predictably conventional, normal, would ever dream of connecting me with the most fabulous multi-spy of all time; a spectacular hero figure, fearless, ruthless, dashing. While, on the perilous margins of society, I was participating in the desperate intrigues and adventures of the international sub-world, juggling identities with superb psychological skill, I would simultaneously present my consistently mediocre façade without a scrap of evidence that I'd ever possessed another.

I was about to become the world's best-kept secret; one that would never be told. What a thrilling enigma for posterity I should be!

OTHER NEW YORK REVIEW CLASSICS

For a complete list of titles, visit www.nyrb.com or write to:
Catalog Requests, NYRB, 435 Hudson Street, New York, NY 10014

* *Also available as an electronic book.*